SADDLEROCK

Just before dawn, five men rode into the small town of Saddlerock to rob the stage of gold bullion. By the time the sun was up, the driver of the stage and the three deputies with him had been shot down and the raiders had made off with their loot. But one man, Matt Turner, was suspected of being the leader of the notorious robbers and was thrown into jail to await trail. Only Slim Hogan, the sheriff of Saddlerock, believed Matt's story that he was innocent . . .

RICK LANDER

SADDLEROCK

Complete and Unabridged

LINFORD
Leicester

First hardcover edition published in
Great Britain in 2002 by
Robert Hale Limited, London

Originally published in paperback as
'Night of the Gunhawk' by Chuck Adams

Second Linford Edition
published 2004

by arrangement with
Robert Hale Limited, London

The moral right of the author has been asserted

British Library CIP Data

Lander, Rick, *1928* –
    Saddlerock.—Large print ed.—
    Linford western library
    1. Western stories
    2. Large type books
    I. Title II. Adams, Chuck. Night of the Gunhawk
    823.9'14 [F]

    ISBN 1–84395–316–1

Published by
F. A. Thorpe (Publishing)
Anstey, Leicestershire

Set by Words & Graphics Ltd.
Anstey, Leicestershire
Printed and bound in Great Britain by
T. J. International Ltd., Padstow, Cornwall

This book is printed on acid-free paper

1

Stage Robbery

It was still dark when the five men rode over the wide river whose bottom was sand and scarcely covered with water. The drought had lasted more than four months in this part of the territory, although the dark thunderheads which had been climbing and building over the western horizon during the night promised rain before long. The smell of the night around them was a blend of baked earth and scorched grass with an overtone of bitter-strong dust that lay heavy in the nostrils.

Three miles north of the town of Saddlerock, they reined their mounts on top of a low rise of bare ground. Behind them there was the faint brightening of the false dawn over the tall hills, peaks spiking the greyness.

One of the men suddenly urged his mount forward, rode a little way ahead of the others, sat easily in the saddle staring out across the dark land which stretched in front of them to where the town slumbered. He was a tall, heavily featured man, black-bearded and hard-eyed, guns wore low in smooth holsters. The men behind him were like him; hard men, scarred with trouble and still wanting trouble.

'You sure that stage will arrive on time, Ed?' grunted one of the men, gigging his horse forward until he sat beside the other.

Ed Chapman's big face became hard. 'They'll be here — and with the gold.' He rubbed the back of a hand over his lips, gave a quick nod. 'An hour after dawn. You all know what to do when the time comes?'

They nodded curtly.

Chapman took cartridges from his belt and pushed them into the chambers of his guns, then thrust them back into the holsters. Sitting there, he ran a dry tongue over equally dry lips, studying the sky through narrowed eyes. Then he swung back to the man beside him. His eyes glittered. 'You got all the evidence we need to pin this on Turner?'

Clayburn nodded briefly, padded the saddlebag beside him. 'It's all here. When we've pulled this job and I've planted this on the scene, they're all going to believe that Matt Turner led the gang that held up the stage in Saddlerock.' He laughed harshly, an ugly sound.

'Good.' Chapman gave a terse nod. The lines around his mouth deepened a little. 'I've been waiting a long time for this. Not just the stage, but getting even with Turner. He turned us in after that last job. I swore then that I'd finish him and if we can lay our hands on a hundred thousand dollars' worth of gold into the bargain, those are the kind of odds I like.'

He lifted his reins, urged his mount forward into the dimness, the rest of the men moving up behind him. Ahead of them, the trail wound between tall columns of red sandstone, then out into the open before it dipped down towards Saddlerock. They crossed another shallow stream which wound past the edge of a ranch, then over a wooden bridge where the echoes were hollow under the hooves of their mounts, and a little while later rode into the main street of Saddlerock.

The town stood on a low shelf of ground with tall hills backing it to the west. To the east lay the flatness of the cattle spreads, now touched by the long drought. The town had been born in the long days of violence which had marked this part of the western frontier of the country. It had never been planned. The railroad had not yet reached it, and the stage line was the only link with the rest of the territory. Men had built the town with guts and sweat, knocking up a store here and a saloon next door to the solitary hotel. The stage station lay towards the eastern end of the main street, standing a hundred yards or so from the sheriff's office which stood on the same side.

The attack on the stage had been well planned. For more than three weeks they had watched as it had pulled up outside the small station, keeping a close check on it from behind the curtained windows of the hotel across the street. Now they knew to the minute when it would arrive in Saddlerock, knew that with this particular shipment the number of guards riding with the stage would be doubled. Everything had been taken care of . . .

* * *

The agent at the stage station was still only half awake. The stage was due in about an hour and the message telling him about its cargo had only reached him the night before. He leaned back in his chair and put his feet up on the desk, yawning a little. Outside, the town was just beginning to wake. It was almost dawn and through the small window he could just make out the grey glow that began to filter along the dusty street. A dull, muted roll of thunder echoed from the west. Vaguely he heard the sound of riders coming along the main street, felt a sense of surprise as they reined outside the station.

The street door opened a moment later and three men came in. Pausing only for a moment, one of them moved towards him and the agent turned his head curiously wondering who would be calling on him at this early hour. Then his right hand reached out sharply for the gun lying on the table in front of him, halted instinctively at the sharp, rough voice:

'Hold it right there,' Chapman ordered curtly. The dim light from the overhead lamp was reflected off the metal of the heavy Colt in his right hand. The barrel was lined directly on the agent's chest and it never wavered. No use to gamble there with his life, although for an instant the thought lived in the other's eyes. Then he shrugged and got slowly to his feet, brows drawn into a hard line over his eyes.

The other two members of the gang came into the office, the linen dusters drawn up over the lower halves of their faces.

'Get his gun,' said Chapman to one of the men, 'then get over to the window and keep a sharp look out along the street in both directions. They may decide to hurry the stage on through this time and we'll have to be ready for it. Besides, the sheriff may figure on coming along to make sure everything is all right.'

'You'll never get away with holding up the stage,' said the agent. 'Besides, there's nothing on it for you to risk your necks and — '

'Keep your mouth shut,' snapped Chapman harshly. 'We know all about that gold bullion they're carrying on this run. If you do as you're told, you may get out of this alive. If not, we'll shoot you now. Make your choice. You're of no use to us.'

This was not strictly true. They needed him for the moment when the stage pulled up outside the office. The deputies riding shotgun would still be wary even though they would never be expecting a hold up inside the town itself and they would need the agent to go outside and allay their fears for the vital moments before they moved in. The agent swallowed nervously at the threat, his adam's apple bobbing up and down in his throat, then he nodded slowly.

'That's better.' Chapman gave a vicious grin. He walked across the room and settled himself comfortably in the chair which the other had just vacated. 'Now you're showing sense. I don't know what they pay you to look after this station, but whatever it is, it ain't worth getting yourself killed for, is it?'

'No, I guess not,' quavered the other. He threw a fearful glance in the direction of the other outlaws as they moved through the office.

'Now we'll just sit here and wait for the stage to arrive.' Chapman eased himself deeper into the chair. The duster over his face was beginning to make him sweat but he knew better than to remove it. In the room the atmosphere was oppressive with the threat of the coming storm. The thunder sounded closer now and he guessed that the driver of the incoming stage might be urging on the horses in an attempt to get into town before the storm broke over the trail.

'Anybody moving out there in the street?' He glanced in the direction of the man by the window.

The other half-turned, shook his head. 'All quiet, so far. We put the horses round the back of the building.'

'It's only a question of time before somebody happens along. They won't bring a shipment like this through without taking precautions in the town.'

Chapman remained silent over a long period after that, leaning forward in the chair, his elbows on his knees. But his eyes watched everything, his ears picking out every little sound in the street outside and the overriding rolls of thunder. Very soon the rain would come, would wash away their trail as they made their getaway into the hills. The storm was something they had not foreseen, but even the weather seemed to be working in their favour. The thought gave him a feeling of grim amusement. He thought of Matt Turner, the man he intended to frame for the robbery, and a twisted smile touched the corners of his thin lips. Earlier he had wanted to destroy Turner in one swift stroke, but now that was not enough. The plan to incriminate him with this robbery had come gradually but the more he had thought about it, the more he had liked it. It had been a simple thing to learn Turner's whereabouts and his plans. He knew that the other had arrived in Saddlerock from back east less than three weeks before and that two days earlier he had ridden out of town into the hills, and would not arrive back there for perhaps two or three more days. When he did ride back into Saddlerock it would be to face a charge of robbery, and as far as the people there were concerned, there was only one punishment for that, particularly as some of the townsfolk would be shot dead during the robbery. Even if they put him in jail pending trial by the circuit judge, it was extremely unlikely that he would remain there. A lynch mob would soon be formed to break him out of jail and string him up from the nearest branch.

He felt an inward sense of pleasure at the thought, but almost immediately his mind jerked itself abruptly to the present as the man over by the window said sharply: 'Somebody heading this way. Could be the sheriff.'

Swiftly he got to his feet and walked across to the window, glancing out cautiously, taking care not to let himself be seen by anyone outside. The man who made his way slowly along the boardwalk was tall, broad-shouldered, with an open, pleasant face. He wore his guns low and looked like a man who knew how to handle them.

Chapman sucked in his lips. 'Don't see any badge, but it could be the sheriff, I reckon. You all know what to do if he decides to come here. Get that agent through into the back room and keep him quiet. If he behaves, we'll let him keep a whole skin, if not — ' He deliberately left the rest of the threat unsaid, knowing that the agent was watching him closely, his eyes wide.

A minute later the agent was in the other room at the rear of the office and the remaining four men had taken up their positions facing the door. Outside the sound of footsteps on the boardwalk grew louder as the man approached the station. They paused almost directly outside the door and Chapman drew himself up tautly to his full height, the gun in his hand trained on the door, where two of his men stood one on either side, ready to slash downward with the butts of their revolvers the moment he gave the signal. He did not particularly want to tangle with the law right now, but if it came, if it could not be avoided, then he was prepared to meet that contingency.

There was the sharp scrape of a match against the outside wall of the stage station, then silence for a long moment. Whoever stood out there was obviously lighting a smoke for himself. If he opened the door and stepped into the office, it would be the last thing he would remember for a long time, Chapman thought grimly.

Then the man stomped away into the distance and the sound of his footsteps faded slowly on the hollow-echoing boardwalk. Chapman let out his breath in short pinches of sound, then lowered the gun in his hand and stared bleakly at the others.

'Stay here,' he ordered brusquely. He checked the old-fashioned clock on the wall. It still wanted another thirty minutes or so before the stage was due. 'I want to have a talk with the agent.'

'You figure there may be trouble?' inquired one of the men over by the door.

'Could be. He may know how many men will be riding with it and whether any fresh orders have been given. If they have, he'll likely have got them last night. They won't have had time to send them through this morning.'

He went into the next room where Clayburn stood lounging against one wall, a Colt held almost negligently in his right hand. The agent was seated on a bare wooden chair in one corner of his room, eyes wide, with a look of terror in them. Quite clearly he did not really believe Chapman when the other had promised that he would be allowed to live provided he did exactly as he was told, and thought that he would be shot down out of hand once the robbery had been staged.

Chapman pulled up one of the other chairs and rested his body in it, elbows over the back, his gaze fixed on the other. Softly he said: 'I figger that you will have had some special orders about this stage. Where are they?'

The man shook his head vehemently. 'I ain't got no orders,' he said thickly. 'All I know is that it'll be here at its usual time. There were no — '

'Don't lie to me.' Chapman's tone took on a sharper edge. 'They wouldn't run a stage through with all of that bullion on board without warning the agents along the route. You must've got those orders last night. There ain't been enough time for you to get 'em this morning. Now, for the last time, where are they?'

He let his gaze slide momentarily in the direction of the man leaning against the wall. Clayburn lifted the nozzle of the Colt menacingly, lining it up on the other's head between the eyes.

The agent licked his lips nervously, shifted his glance from one man to the other. Then his shoulders sagged and he said in a voice that was little more than a husky whisper: 'In the other room, in the drawer of the desk.'

'That's better. Now you're being sensible.' Chapman heaved himself to his feet, went through into the outer room, throwing a swiftly appraising glance at the clock on the wall. Another fifteen minutes or so and the stage would be due in Saddlerock. He forced a grim smile, walked over to the desk and opened the drawer. The agent had not lied. The orders were there on a single sheet of paper. He ran his gaze over them swiftly. Three deputies would be riding with the stage, together with the driver. Evidently the authorities were not anticipating too much trouble otherwise they would have doubled that number of men riding with the bullion. Possibly they had figured that too many deputies riding shotgun would arouse suspicion and advertise the fact that there was something of importance being carried.

There was a sudden thunder on the roof of the building and a moment later the rain came. Outside in the street the heavy drops lifted tiny funnels of dust which were quickly turned into a literal sea of mud. Lightning forked the heavens and thunder cracked savagely overhead. Within moments it was as if a curtain had suddenly descended over everything.

There would be no let up for the rest of the day, Chapman mused. It would be hard riding once they made their getaway out of town, and uncomfortable, but he and the men with him had rode wet before and, with all of that gold in their saddlebags, he doubted if any of them would feel like complaining.

'Keep your eyes peeled now,' he warned the men at the window. 'That stage could come at any time and the law may decide to appear.'

'There are a few folk moving around further along the street,' grunted one of the men. 'Reckon this rain ought to keep most of 'em indoors unless they got any real cause to be out.'

Chapman gave a quick nod, went into the other room. He threw the agent a sharp glance. 'That stage ought to be due in a few minutes,' he said with an ominously quiet voice. 'When it gets here you go out as if nothing was wrong. Get me?'

The man swallowed heavily and forced a quick nod.

'Good. I don't want to have to kill you, but if you make me, I will.'

There was a sudden yell from the other room. Swiftly Chapman went through. Beside the window one of the men turned and said quickly: 'Looks like the sheriff heading this way, boss.'

Swiftly Chapman moved over to the window. The tall figure walking swiftly in their direction did not pause but continued to come along the boardwalk, with the rain dripping from the brim of the wide hat he wore. As he got closer Chapman noticed the silver star on the other's shirt, gave a quick nod. 'He's heading this way all right,' he muttered grimly. 'No shooting though until the stage gets here. We don't want to warn all of the town. Let him come in through the door and then knock him cold. By the time he comes round we'll be miles away in the hills.'

'Clayburn.' He called the other's name softly.

'Yeah, boss?' The outlaw's answer came instantly.

'Bring the agent through here.'

Within moments the agent had been thrust through into the room, with Clayburn standing at his back, the muzzle of his Colt pushed deep into the man's spine, ready to choke off any wrong move the other might try to make once the sheriff appeared on the scene.

One of the outlaws took up his position on the side of the room near the door, waited with the Colt held tightly in his right hand. The heavy footsteps halted immediately outside the door and a second later there came a knock.

'You ready for the stage, Walter?'

called a loud voice.

'All right,' hissed Chapman thinly, 'answer him. Tell him to come on inside.'

The agent stepped forward nervously as Chapman moved over, out of sight of anyone coming in the door.

'Sure, Sheriff. I'm ready. Come on inside.'

The door opened. There was a brief pause, then the tall figure of the sheriff stepped into the room. He gave a quick nod, then seemed to sense there was something wrong, for his hand moved towards the gun in his belt, his body half turning as he tried to drag the weapon clear of the holster. He had it half clear when the heavy butt of the Colt caught him on the back of the skull, pitching him forward on to his face.

Chapman bent over the sheriff for a moment, then gave a quick nod of satisfaction. 'Drag him through into the other room and tie his hands and feet, just in case he comes round sooner than we expect. We don't want him stepping into things at the wrong moment.'

Scarcely was this done than there was a sound of horses approaching at a gallop from the far end of town.

'Here they come,' said one, 'right on time.'

'Good. You all know what to do.' Chapman tightened the duster across the lower half of his features. Thrusting the agent towards the door he jerked it open, stood to one side, his body screened by the other. 'Now, no tricks, mind,' he said viciously. 'The first wrong move you make, and you'll be a dead man.'

The stage had entered the main street of the town now, was coming quickly in the direction of the stage station, the driver leaning forward in the teeming rain, using the whip over the horses. The stage swayed ominously from side to side in the churned up mud of the street, the wooden wheels throwing muddy water in all directions.

Chapman edged forward a little, noticed that there was only one man riding on the seat with the driver. The other two, he reflected, would be inside the coach with the bullion. That complicated matters a little.

Twenty seconds later the stage pulled up outside the station. The driver yelled something, hitched up the reins to the seat and made to swing his legs down. Beside him the man riding shotgun, a grim-faced man, let his gaze swing idly over to the doorway. Chapman threw a quick look along the street, saw that in the teeming rain it was empty, then stepped out into the open, feet braced apart on the boardwalk, the Colts in his hands covering the two men on the top of the stage.

'All right, hold it right there,' he called loudly. 'Lower your guns, driver, and you with the rifle, drop it on the ground.'

Even as he spoke, he gestured with his left hand to the other men inside the office. They came rushing out into the street, two men on either side of the stage, reaching for the doors and pulling them open, Colts in their hands.

Out of the corner of his eye, Chapman saw the agent, suddenly plucking up his courage, moving back towards the open door of the office. Even as he swung towards the other, the man with the shotgun made a swift move, lowering the weapon in a blur of motion, finger tightening on the trigger. Before he could loose off a shot, the guns in Chapman's hands roared and the man pitched out of his seat, hitting the street with a sickening thud, a deep red stain already beginning to spread over his shirt.

Inside the doorway the agent had stopped, eyes turned towards the man in the street, his body close to the stamping hooves of the horses. There seemed to be no further fight left in him.

Another full volley rang out as the two deputies inside the stage opened up, crouching down behind the doors.

The two outlaws fired shot after shot into the stage, backing away a little. Chapman heard one of the men die; he heard death come distinctly as a rough tearing impact of lead through wood and clothing and flesh, followed by a grunt and a low sigh. The man fell against the inside of the stage door and it opened under his weight, spilling him limply out into the street.

Almost before his body hit the mud his companion died as more slugs tore into him from the other side. Chapman glanced up, saw that the driver had also been hit, was lying slumped over the driving seat, arms hanging limply forward. Whether he was dead or not he did not know, but there was no time to find out. The shooting would have aroused the whole of the town by now and the sooner they picked up the bullion and got away, the better.

The others had already pulled the two heavy boxes from inside the stage and two swift shots shattered the locks on each. Each man knew exactly what to do. Two minutes after the first shot had been fired, the gold had been loaded into the saddlebags and the strongboxes were empty, the teeming rain already beginning to fill them with a filming of water.

Chapman ran for his mount standing in the narrow alleyway beside the stage station. He heard the vicious hum of a bullet, fired from somewhere along the street, scorch the air close to his head as he ran, knew that there was little time to spare. So far everything had gone accordingly to the plan they had worked out. Every muscle in him began to ache as he swung himself up into the saddle. The rain dripped from the brim of his hat into his eyes, making it difficult to see properly. His mind was now very clear and sharp. Every single sound around him seemed to have been magnified so that he could hear it clearly. There was some confused shouting at the far end of the street and the voices seemed to be coming nearer. A rifle blasted savagely from the other side of the main street from one of the windows near the hotel and a slug thudded into the wooden wall of the building behind him as he urged his mount forward, crouching low in the saddle, to present a more difficult target.

The rest of his men were already saddled up. Swiftly they dug their spurs into the flanks of their mounts and raced out of town, the rain falling swiftly and steadily around them. Behind them, Chapman heard the harsh cry of the road agent, but the sound was soon lost as they rode out of Saddlerock and headed swiftly along the rocky trail which led them north towards the hill, vaguely seen through the curtain of rain and the vivid flashes of the lightning that lanced and spiked the beserk heavens as the storm closed in around them in its full fury.

Slim Hogan, sheriff of Saddlerock, rubbed the back of his head tenderly, wincing as his fingers touched the place where he had been slugged. There was a grim, tight expression on his features.

'Anybody see those hombres when they rode outa town?' he gritted, turning his head slowly and staring at the small crowd that had gathered in the pouring rain, their eyes fixed on the men lying sprawled beside the stage.

The men shook their heads in silence. Finally one spoke up. 'They must've been in the station long afore the stage got here, Sheriff.' A musing edge came into his voice. 'I heard one of them yell somethin' as they rode off and I reckon I've heard that voice somewheres before.'

Hogan whirled on him almost savagely. 'Better remember where it was you heard it then, Chet. Those outlaws killed my brother and I mean to get every last one of 'em if it takes me the rest of my life.'

The other rubbed his chin thoughtfully, shuffled his feet a trifle nervously in the wet mud of the street. His clothing sagged wetly against his body. 'It could've been in the hotel. Sure, that's where I heard that voice before. There were three of 'em then. They put up in the hotel coupla days back. You figure they were there spyin' out the land, checking on the movements of the stage?'

'Could be,' broke in the agent. He wiped the back of his hand across his eyes as the rain began to drip into them. 'They seemed to know a lot about the stage and about the orders that came through for me last night.'

'Makes sense,' agreed Hogan. He walked over and motioned to one of the men to come forward. 'We'll get Ben's body into the station. Then you'd better get the others inside. Reckon we'll have to have the coroner told.'

'You figgering on getting a posse together and riding out after them murderin' polecats?' asked the agent.

'Ain't much point going after them right now,' muttered the sheriff. 'The rain will have washed away their trail within minutes, and once they get into the hills we'd never locate them. We'll wait until the storm blows itself out and then ride out and see if we can pick 'em up. But if Chet heard that voice in the hotel, it gives us something to go on. Somebody else in town may have seen somebody suspicious.'

'What about that gun we found in the alley back there?' inquired another of the men. 'One of those critters must've dropped it when they rode out. There's some initials on the butt. Could mean somethin'.'

'Hand it over,' muttered Hogan. He took the Colt from the other and turned it over in his hands several times, glancing down at the crudely cut letters in the butt.

'M.T.' he said quietly. 'Anyone here know of a hombre with those initials?'

'Matt Turner,' answered Chet promptly. 'He rode into town a few days ago and put up at the hotel. Reckon we ought to go along there and check on him, mebbe ask him a few questions.'

'I'll do the asking around here,' said Hogan tightly. There was a bright, speculative glint in his eyes. 'But you could be right. I always thought there might be something a mite suspicious about him. Never said much about himself except that he rode in from some place back east.' He turned his head and stared musingly along the street, through the curtain of pouring rain, in the direction of the hotel where it stood head and shoulders above every other building on that side of the street.

While the men carried the other bodies into the stage station, Hogan walked along the wetly shining boardwalk, then crossed over the street to the hotel, pushing open the door and striding purposefully inside. The clerk behind the desk glanced up curiously, then relaxed as soon as he saw who it was.

Expectantly, he said: 'I heard some shooting a while back, Sheriff. Any trouble?'

'Plenty!' said Hogan curtly. 'Some outlaw gang were waiting in the stage station, holding up Hank at gunpoint.

They robbed the stage after shooting down the driver and three deputies.'

A look of surprise spread over the clerk's face, then it changed to one of sudden concern and realisation. 'But Ben was riding with — '

Hogan nodded tightly. 'That's right, Ben was one of the deputies they shot down. Now you can realise why I'm going to ask a lot of questions and then I mean to get a posse together and we're going to track down that gang and bring them all in, dead or alive.'

'But why come here, Sheriff?' asked the other. He leaned forward over the desk, perplexed.

'Chet reckons he recognised one of the men from the way he spoke. They were all wearing dusters so nobody got a look at their faces. But he reckons he heard one of 'em here in the hotel a coupla days ago. You got any records in the register of anybody staying here? There's that hombre Turner. We'd like to have a talk with him if you'll give me his room number.'

The clerk was in the act of swivelling the register on the desk in front of him and paused quickly.

'I'm afraid Mr. Turner isn't at the hotel, Sheriff.'

Hogan glanced up. 'You mean he's pulled out?'

'Not exactly. He left two days ago, said he had business in Tucson but that he wanted us to keep his room for him, that he'd be back in five days or so. He left his baggage there and paid in advance.' He drew his brows together into a tight line. 'You don't reckon he was one of that gang, do you?'

'It's beginning to look mighty like it,' retorted the sheriff. 'Seems funny he should have left just before this robbery took place, and if he was here as you say, he'd have had plenty of opportunity to keep a close watch on the stage station from the window of the hotel. Reckon I'll step up to his room and take a look around.'

'Help yourself, Sheriff.' The other reached behind him and plucked a key from the rack, held it out. 'You'll find his room at the top of the stairs, at the end of the passage on the left.'

'Thanks.' Hogan took the key and made his way swiftly up the wide stairs. Inside the room he looked about him, went over to the window and glanced out to satisfy himself that it was possible to see the station from the room. Then he went through the drawers in the room. He could find nothing suspicious there, although he had not really expected anything of that nature. If Turner was in that gang of outlaws, then he would have covered his tracks well, leaving nothing to be upturned. Turner's bag was on the floor near the chest of drawers and he opened it, tipped the contents on to the bed. There was nothing but a couple of shirts and a rolled-up pair of pants. He pushed them back into the bag and replaced it, then went out of the room, locking the door behind him.

Behind the desk, the clerk lifted his brows slightly as he took the key back.

'Find anything, Sheriff?' he asked.

Hogan shook his head. 'I didn't really expect to.'

'You reckon he'll be coming back if he was riding with that gang?'

'He might. Could be he'll figure that nobody will connect him with the robbery if he comes riding back into town.'

By the time Hogan reached the street the stage was being moved into the alley at the side of the station. Most of the small crowd had dissipated. The rain was still coming down in sheets, water flooding from one side of the street to the other. The stage agent stood inside the open doorway, peering unhappily out. He straightened as the sheriff came over, brushing the rain out of his eyes.

'Find anythin' over there, Sheriff?'

'Nothing definite. He could be one of that gang. If he is and he comes riding back, we'll take him, make him give us the names of the others and their hideout in the hills.'

The other glanced sideways at the Sheriff.

'What you got in mind, Slim?'

'Well, it seems they must've been watching the stage office for some time until they had the times of the stage arriving and leaving. They must've ridden into town from the east, that means they'd know just when the stage was due this morning, and once they hogtied you here, they'd soon know how you'd have special orders and that would be all they needed. They knew they could rely on you to help 'em if you had a gun in your back and they were ready for me the minute I went inside the door.'

'Then if they're heading for the hills, there are only two trails they can take. One passes close to Moreno's ranch. We could see if he heard anything during the morning.'

'And if he didn't, then you reckon they must have taken the north trail and that goes nowhere near any place.' Hogan shook his head slowly. 'That at once lessens our chances of ever finding them so long as they stay holed up in there. There must be a hundred Indian trails in the hills and twice that number of places where men could hole up for several weeks. I reckon it seems a cinch they'll stay there until they reckon the heat is off. Then they might try to make a break for Tucson or one of the other big towns to the east. It won't be easy to get rid of gold bullion. Notes — yes, but gold isn't the easiest thing to dispose of.'

For some time the agent was silent, a worried frown on his grizzled features. When he did not speak, the sheriff went on slowly: 'There's another reason I'm not too keen on taking a posse up there into the hills right now. I don't like taking the chance of getting more men killed, 'cause once any of that gang gets a man in their sights, they'll never give him a chance to put a gun on them. There won't be any mistake about that and to ride up into those hills even though we know them reasonably well ourselves, is asking for trouble. There are so many places where men could ambush us, drop us in our saddles before we even knew they were there.'

'So we wait for Turner to come riding back into a trap. Is that it?'

'That's the general idea,' nodded Hogan. 'I know how folk feel in this town about what has happened. My own brother was one of those men killed, riding with the stage. I've got more right than anyone else in this town to go out hunting down those killers. But there's no sense in going off half-cock over this and a slug or two of lead inside a few of the townsfolk won't build up any enthusiasm for capturin' outlaws.'

2

Showdown

The sun beat down on the desert country with a fiery and inextinguishable intensity, burning and drying the ground until it had been caked here and there with deep cracks forming along the dried-up bed of a river, now with only the smooth, shiny stones visible, gleaming fiercely in the hot light. By the middle of the morning the slight film of moisture which had fallen during the cold night had either been sucked up or drawn out by the blistering heat of the sun. The stunted bushes seemed to have been withered almost as soon as they had sprung up and now lived only by the slenderest thread, their deep roots avidly sucking what little moisture they could out of the parched ground.

A little after high noon, the heat expanded and became more oven-like and Matt Turner rode slowly with his body bent forward a little, head well down so that the wide brim of his hat shielded his head and eyes from the vicious, savage glare of the sunlight that flooded everything around him for as far as the eye could see.

He had wandered off the trail some time during the latter half of the night, and although he knew that it lay somewhere to the south of him, he was not quite certain how far away it lay and he did not wish to keep turning his slow-moving mount in that direction just on the chance that he might have been mistaken and such a move would actually take him even further from the trail and deeper into the Badlands.

Once in there, moving slowly to the north where there would be no water for miles and very little shade, it would not be long before a man and his mount died. Lifting his head a little, he slitted his eyes against the sun glare and tried to make out any sign of Saddlerock on the horizon, but there were only the occasional dust devils, spinning and whirling along his line of vision, so that the skyline seemed to shimmer and shake as if it lay behind a layer of dark water.

This was bad, tainted country, he thought to himself. He did not know this country at all and he did not like it. The monotonous expanse of yellow-white alkali and the rising buttes of red sandstone which stood out like grim and evil sentinels all around him, tall and barren in the desert, seemed frightening and terrible. There were no animals here, nothing that moved. It was as if the glaring disc of the sun looked down on an endless world of white heat with only himself crawling with an infinite slowness across it. He had been riding since shortly after midnight, hoping to make time during the cold starlit darkness of the night before the sun came up and brought with it the intolerable heat. But dawn had found him still many miles from town and now, after midday, the heat was hot and agonising, forcing itself behind his eyes, striking his body forcibly. He rode steadily but did not attempt to push his horse. That could easily be a fatal mistake in country like this. The feel of the horse under him did a little to ease the tenseness, the ache in his body.

Moistening his parched lips with the tip of his tongue, he felt for the water bottle at his hip, held it up to his ear and shook it slowly. The faint swirl and splash of the water in it told him that it was less than half full now and he would not cross another stream until he came within sight of Saddlerock. Crooked eyes scanned the never-ending face of the desert. Although to anyone watching he would have appeared half asleep, with his eyes slitted and scarcely an expression on his face, there was still an awareness in him, something which was constantly there.

The previous afternoon, when he was

one day's ride out from Tucson, he had spotted a dust cloud over to his right, knew that a bunch of riders were moving swiftly by on another trail. But they had swerved across to the north and had moved on and away and he had never known who they were nor why they were pushing their mounts so hard in the desert. Either they had been heading into trouble or running away from it, he mused slowly.

The heat had increased during the long hours of the afternoon, but a little before dark, with the shadows riding long in front of him and the sun dropping into the west in a burst of red-edged flame, he came on to the main trail once more and breathed more easily.

As he rode the terrain changed slowly. It became more rugged, with clumps of stunted trees closing in on him from every side. The world changed, became blue and still and there was the smell of the hills in his nostrils as the faint breeze grew stronger and the more pronounced against his face. He crossed a shallow creek, then put the tired horse to a climbing section of the trail, riding between tall mounds of rock that rose up on either side before he started the roundabout ride into the bench-lands.

The cool breeze flowed against him, taking the heat from his body. He could now sit up tall and straight in the saddle, open his eyes without having to face the searing glare of the sunlight, easing the ache in the lower half of his body, an ache brought on over the long hours by being forced to sit crouched over in the saddle.

The horse increased its gait as they came within sight of the town. Saddle-rock lay on a low bench of land, rising up slightly from the surrounding desert country. A plank bridge carried over the upper reaches of the shallow river and he noticed that here it had been swollen by recent rains, the dull, muddy water rushing swiftly by under the bridge. The sound of his horse's hooves reached him hollowly as he passed over it. Then he entered the main street of Saddlerock. On either side the squat, single-storied houses stood silent in the dimness of evening, and behind them were other buildings scattered throughout the blue dusk.

Even as he rode into town he had the feeling that there was something wrong. For a long moment he eased off the forward movement of the horse and sat tall and taut in the saddle, peering about him. The odd feeling of impending trouble persisted. It was nothing he could put his finger on, but nevertheless it was there and it bothered him. Perhaps it was the fact that although lights showed yellowly through the windows of several of the houses fronting on to the street and the hotel and saloons seemed crowded as usual, there were too few people on the street itself. And those he did see soon turned and moved back into the shadows as he rode past, eyeing him curiously for a moment, then with a hardening look on their faces which he noticed quite clearly.

Halfway along the main street another narrower one cut down from the direction of the hills and intersected it, forming a square. It was around this square that the saloons and hotel had been built.

He bit his lip indecisively. There was something wrong here and he had the inescapable feeling that he had ridden right into the middle of it. If only he knew what it was, he might have felt a little easier in his mind. As it was, he could sense the tension beginning to crackle in the dimness of the dusk.

His mount began to fidget, chomping at the bit between its teeth, occasionally lifting its head, nostrils flared, to smell the breeze blowing in off the distant hills. Down there at the far end of the street there was the usual rack going on outside the saloon. From where he sat, it seemed quite innocuous. Yet there was that undercurrent of menace flowing about him, as invisible and yet as tangible as the breeze. Tension continued to grow in him as he gigged his mount forward. Something had happened here during the five days he had been away and his alertness grew as sharp as the honed edge of a hunting knife. Eyes flicked from side to side, probing the shadows of the boardwalk, under the wooden overhangs of the buildings. Tall in the saddle, he rode like a cavalry man, loose-limbed, right hand hanging down by his side, just touching the pommel of the saddle with his fingertips.

Behind him, in the growing darkness of the encroaching night, silence lived at his back. In front of the sheriff's office, he saw Slim Hogan step out through the open doorway and stand against one of the wooden uprights. He rolled himself a smoke, keeping his gaze on the man riding slowly along the street. Matt saw the other strike a sulphur match until the sulphur had burned off the tip and apply the light to the end of his cigarette, blowing smoke into the air in front of him.

Matt studied the other in the dim light as he drew level with the sheriff. Hogan continued to stare up at him and he thought he detected a look of curious appraisal on the sheriff's features, as if he were inwardly trying to make up his mind about something.

That spot in the middle of his back began to ache again as if there was a gun somewhere behind him, already lined up on his shoulder blades, with an itching finger on the trigger. He tried to ignore it but the feeling grew as he edged his mount past the sheriff, aware that the other still continued to watch him with that oddly perplexed look.

His nervousness increased. He was like an animal now. Danger was there and it seemed to have sharpened his instincts, and he realised that his mount was apprehensive, too, head turning from side to side.

Suddenly he noticed the small knot of men who had come pushing out of the nearest saloon. They stood on the boardwalk, their hands very near their guns and there was a menace in the way they watched him.

One of them he recognised as Chet Wainwright suddenly yelled harshly: 'There he is, Sheriff. Why don't you shoot him down like he shot your brother? Why are you letting him ride on?'

Matt whirled swiftly in the saddle. His right hand dropped instinctively for the gun at his belt, but he froze instantly as Hogan's voice at his back snapped: 'Don't try to draw that gun, Turner. Just sit quite still right where you are, or I'll shoot you in the back.'

For a moment Matt sat stock still in the saddle, scarcely able to believe his ears. There was no denying the intensity of the anger in the sheriff's tone, and he knew that the other meant every word he said.

Slowly he lifted his hands, keeping them well away from his sides. Out of the corner of his eye he saw the bunch of men come down the steps into the street, then move towards him with a singleness of purpose that sent a little shiver moving like a finger of ice along his spine.

Hogan moved around into view in front of him, the Colt trained on his chest. His lips were compressed into a tight line across the middle of his features.

Chet Wainwright came forward. He grinned sourly, 'Never figgured he'd come ridin' back into town as bold as this, Sheriff,' he said sharply. He looked up at Matt. 'Man, you must be plumb crazy to reckon you could pull a job like that and then come riding back.'

'Now jest a minute — ' began Matt harshly. He looked from one man to the other. 'At least you can tell me straight jest what it is I'm bein' accused of doing. What job are you talking about?'

Wainwright laughed thinly, turned to the other men standing at his back. 'Listen to him, boys. Holds up the stage, shoots down three men with that gang of his and then wants to know

49

what it is he's done.'

The men guffawed harshly, nodded their heads quickly. But before Matt could speak, could protest his innocence, Hogan chimed in: 'Just let me do all of the talking here, Chet. We ain't got no proper proof that he was one of those outlaws.' He switched his gaze to Matt. 'Better step down from that horse, Turner, and don't make any quick moves towards those guns of yours, or I'll forget I'm the law around here and pull this trigger.'

Slowly Matt swung his legs and dropped lightly from the saddle. The deep weariness that had been in his body during the long, hot ride across the desert was gone now, lost in amazement at what was happening.

Reaching forward, the sheriff plucked the twin Colts from his holsters, let them drop into the dirt. Then he relaxed and lowered the muzzle of the gun he held on him.

'That's better. Now I reckon you'd better come along with me, Turner.

Walk back to the jail.' The star on the other's chest gleamed dully in the faint light. Several men and women standing on the boardwalk moved aside to let them pass and there was no doubting the hostility on their faces.

Every nerve and muscle tense, Matt moved ahead of the sheriff. His mind whirling, trying to figure out some answer to this. The men had spoken of a stage robbery. Presumably this had happened in town while he had been away, and yet they had connected him with it. He shook his head slowly. He could find no answer to it at the moment. Perhaps Sheriff Hogan might be able to furnish him with some explanation once they reached the office.

'Nerve of him, riding back into town like that,' muttered a man from one of the doorways. 'You ought to shoot him down right now, Sheriff. Save us all the expense of a trial.'

Hogan said nothing but continued to prod him forward with the muzzle of the gun.

'Murderin', thievin' sidewinder,' snarled another.

'Get a rope and we'll hang him now,' called a third voice, a little more authoritative than the others.

Turner glanced up and saw that they had almost drawn level with the door of the sheriff's office, but out of the corner of his eye he saw more of the men moving forward, some heading towards them from the other side of the street, and there was the unmistakable sound of riders edging their mounts slowly forward from behind him. There was something ominous and threatening in these sounds and he swallowed thickly. At the door of the office Matt held still, with the sheriff close at his back.

He saw a man step forward with a rope held loosely in his hands, the end shaped into a noose, swinging slightly as he dangled it towards the ground, trailing it in the dust.

Hogan turned and faced the hostile crowd. 'I'm taking Turner in on suspicion of being involved in that stage hold-up a coupla days ago,' he said quietly. 'He ain't been proved to have been one of those sidewinders, but if he is, then I reckon we ought to be able to hold him until the circuit judge gets here week after next, and once we've tried him and he's been found guilty, then we know what to do with him. But every man's entitled to a fair trial in this territory.'

'Ain't you forgetting the kind of man he is, Sheriff?' asked Chet Wainwright. He pushed his way to the front of the threatening crowd and stood alongside the man with the noosed rope in his hands. There was a look of dark anger on his face. 'He shot down your brother, Hogan. We know that he was in that gang. We found his gun near the scene of the hold-up and I recognised his voice. What more proof do you want than that?'

'Plenty!' snapped Hogan. 'You're right, Chet, when you say that he may be the man leading that gang of outlaws, and I reckon that I have more right than any of you to see him dead. But I'm the law here and I say that we have to do this thing according to the law. If we were to shoot down every man we suspect of being in a gang of robbers, then there'd soon be no law and order in the territory at all.'

'Law and order,' snapped the other darkly. His eyes met Matt's and the other felt stunned at the hatred in them. 'You stopped to figger what his cronies are likely to be doing while you're holding him here in jail until Judge Parker gits here?'

'Suppose you tell me?' muttered Hogan.

'Ain't it obvious? They'll soon git to know we're holding him and they'll come ridin' into town and bust him outa jail. Is that what you want?'

'Now hold on there,' Hogan said. 'I ain't going to let this man be strung up without a proper trial jest because you reckon there's a chance of him being busted outa jail. If he is in with them coyotes and they decide to come for him, then we'll get 'em. It'll save us the trouble of getting a posse together and riding out to look for 'em.'

Matt held still, watching the sheriff, who had now moved around to stand beside him. The other held the Colt in his right hand but it was no longer pointed directly at him. It was almost as if Hogan considered the most danger to come from the hostile crowd itself rather than from him.

'I don't know anythin' about any hold-up,' he said tightly, turning his head slightly to face the crowd. 'If it happened here in Saddlerock, I don't see how you could connect it with me. I was in Tucson until the day before yesterday, and no man can ride across that desert out there in less than two days. You know that for yourselves.'

'Ain't no use in denying it, mister,' snapped Wainwright. 'We got you cold.' His little close-set eyes were almost lost behind the puffy cheeks.

'I never took part in any hold-up,' Matt repeated, 'and I don't know anything about the shooting of the sheriff's brother. If anybody here says I did it, then they're lyin'. Somebody seems to be trying to frame me with this holdup.'

'That's jest what we expected you to say, Turner,' muttered one of the men in crowd. 'I made the coffins for those three deputies and the driver, I reckon it won't be no trouble to make one for you.'

'We'll take care of the others if they come riding into town,' murmured another man. 'I reckon we know how to take care of this one now that he's been stupid enough to ride back into our hands.'

'Get that rope of yours, Hank, and we'll string him up right now,' shouted a shrill voice from somewhere at the back of the crowd.

'Now you keep out of this.' Hogan stepped forward a couple of paces and stood on the edge of the boardwalk. 'We ain't going to have any lynching party in Saddlerock. You all know that

I've got no call to protect this man, but he's entitled to speak in his own defence. Once we've proved him guilty, then you'll be able to take him and string him up. Believe me, if he was riding with those rattlers, he'll swing on the end of that rope of yours, Hank.'

There was grumbling among those nearby, but Hogan still held the Colt rock steady in his right hand, and finally the small crowd began to disperse. Matt watched them as they moved off into the darkness along the street. One by one they moved into the saloons, or saddled up and rode out of town. But there were two men, he noticed, who did not leave with the others, but merely walked over to the opposite side of the street where they took up positions on the boardwalk, seated in the wooden chairs, their legs perched on the rail, watching the sheriff's office without any let-up as Hogan turned and said harshly:

'All right, Turner, get inside!' He

walked behind Matt into the office, held the gun on him with one hand while he struck a match and lit the paraffin lamp on the desk with the other. Then he went back and closed the door, locking it and slipping the key into his pocket.

Looking round, he said in a thinly edged tone: 'Don't start getting any ideas from what I said out there, Turner, I'm only hoping that while you're here you'll do something, make some move, that'll give me the excuse to shoot you down so that it won't be on my conscience.'

Matt swallowed, looked the other squarely in the eye. 'You really reckon that I was with that bunch of outlaws who held up the stage and shot your brother, Sheriff?'

'All I know are the facts that I have.' The other bent and opened one of the drawers of the desk, then pulled out a Colt and tossed it on to the top of the desk. 'That your gun?'

Matt didn't need to have the weapon

in his hands to know instinctively that it was his. The gun was one which he had left in his bag in the hotel room before he had left. Part of the plot became clear to him now. Someone, quite obviously one of the outlaws who had carried out the robbery, had taken that gun from his bag and left it at the scene of the crime in a deliberate attempt to incriminate him. But why? He tried to figure out a reason for it, but he could think of none. Surely there was no one in the town who knew him, who bore him that kind of grudge. He had only been in Saddlerock for a little while and had made few friends there and few enemies. No denial of his was going to be believed now, he thought tightly.

'Let me see the gun,' he said thinly.

He took it as the sheriff held it out, noticing that the chambers had been emptied. Evidently the other was still taking no chances as far as he was concerned.

'Well, is it yours?'

'It sure looks like mine,' he admitted slowly. 'Got my initials on the butt. I had one like this, left it in my bag at the hotel before I rode out. Somebody could've gone into my room and stolen it. Then left it at the scene of the robbery so as to incriminate me.'

'Any reason why they should have done that, why they should have picked on you?' There was a note of disbelief in the sheriff's tone as he took the gun back.

'Nope. I guess not. I don't know many folk here in Saddlerock, only been here a coupla weeks.'

'There were other things, too, found there which tie in with you. This neckerchief was found inside the stage station. Wainwright says he seen you wearing it in the hotel just before you upped and left.'

Matt looked down and nodded slowly. The evidence and the accusation were damning. Whoever had wanted to frame him with the robbery and these murders had done a good job of it. He could see no way out. He did not wonder that everyone in the street outside had felt certain he had been the leader of that outlaw band. He felt stunned. It was doubtful if he could even prove he had been in Tucson. There had been few people who had seen him there and scarcely anyone who would remember him.

Hogan said impatiently: 'I reckon you'd better move along to the cells.' He jerked the muzzle of the Colt towards the door on the far side of the room. 'Through there.'

Slowly, wearily, Matt moved towards the door, opened it and stepped through into the passage beyond. Suddenly he felt the weakness come. It crept up swiftly from the pit of his stomach and made his head swim dizzily, contracting the muscles of his throat.

Hogan opened the door of one of the cells, waited until he had gone through and then slammed it behind him, turning the heavy key in the lock. Only then did he pocket the key and thrust the gun back into its holster.

'Sheriff!' Matt called as the other made to turn and retrace his steps along the passage.

'Well?' Coldly, Hogan stared at him through the bars of the cell, only the faint light from the open door at the other end lighting his features.

'When did this hold up take place?'

'You still trying to claim you don't know?'

'That's right. All I know is that I've been out to Tucson and I only got back to Saddlerock this evening. I don't know yet how those things of mine got to the stage station, but it seems to me there's somebody who wants me to take the blame for this, somebody who wants me out of the way. Not only did they want to rob the stage, but they seem determined to have me incriminated.'

'You said that before,' put in the other, 'but you ain't got any idea who it could be. Not much to go on, is it?' The hardness still had not left his tone.

'Maybe not, but there won't be any chance for me to find out if I'm kept here, and if that lynch mob comes to bust me outa jail and string me up, there won't be much you can do stop 'em.'

'They won't make any trouble. Wainwright's all mouth. He talks a lot and does nothing.'

'But if they do decide to come this time,' Matt persisted. 'They seemed pretty heated up out there.'

'Then I'll be ready for 'em,' snapped the other impatiently. He spun on his heel and walked away. Matt sat on the edge of the low bunk against the wall and listened with only a part of his mind to the other's footsteps as they faded into the distance. The door at the far end of the passage was slammed shut and then there was only silence and darkness in the cell.

After a moment he got heavily to his feet and moved across to the other wall, feeling upward until his hands just managed to touch the bottom ledge of the solitary window. His fingertips slid along the lower halves of the steel bars set in it and he knew, with a sudden sinking sensation in his chest, that there would be no way out for him that way. Perhaps there would be men watching that side of the jailhouse anyway, just waiting and hoping that he was going to try to make a break for it. Then they would shoot him down in the street and it would save them from having to take him out and string him up from the nearest convenient branch.

For a long moment he stood there in the darkness, head thrown back as he stared out through the small square of the window, saw the stars glittering brightly in the dark velvet of the night sky. Then the sickness came over him again and he went back quickly to the bunk and stretched himself out on it, surrendering himself to the weariness that lay deep in his tired, beaten body.

The past two weeks had been too much — the long, terrible ride across that stretching desert and then riding into town to discover that he was a wanted man, that he was suspected of being in league with a gang of outlaws and of having shot down the men guarding the stage.

How long he lay there, sunk deep in thought, he did not know, but a sound outside the cell suddenly roused him and he sat up, taut and straight on the bunk. There was a low mutter of sound from somewhere far down the street and a second later a couple of shots were fired, the echoes shuddering away into the silence. Some of the men in the saloons, he guessed, a few of them drunk, but the others still sober enough to know what they were doing. He had the sudden conviction that the lynching party was still prepared to go through with the threat which had been made; that they were afraid he was a member of that outlaw gang and there was the chance of the others riding into town to free him. He strained his ears in an attempt to guess whether they were headed in his direction or not, standing there close to the wall of the cell, scarcely daring to breathe.

Somebody yelled something in a harsh tone. It was not possible for him to make out the words, but it was answered almost immediately by another shout, and then another. Now there was no longer any doubt in his mind that the men were heading in the direction of the jail. He sucked in a deep breath and moved over to the door of the cell, yelling with all of his might.

'You in there, Sheriff?'

There was a moment of silence, and then Hogan's voice reached him from the outer office. 'Keep quiet in there, Turner.'

'That lynch mob is headed this way, Sheriff,' he called back. 'You figuring on leaving me locked in here to die?'

'I'll handle them.' He thought he heard the scrape of a chair being pushed back. 'You keep your mouth shut.'

Angrily, Matt bit his lower lip,

released his tight-fisted hold on the bars of the cell and fought to control the flame of anger that began to burn brightly at the back of his brain. There was no point in trying to do anything foolish at the moment, he told himself fiercely. Maybe Sheriff Hogan could stop those men out there. It was unlikely they would try to go against him. But then there was the chance that if they were sufficiently riled and angry at what had happened, sincerely believing that he had been riding with that gang, then they would ignore anything Hogan tried to say when he tried to reason with them, and would come busting into the jail, take him out and string him up, with Hogan unable to do anything to stop them.

The tightness grew in his mind as he stood there, peering into the darkness of the passage beyond the barred door, trying to pick out every little sound going on outside the jail. He heard a couple of men go riding past. They did not halt their mounts, but continued to ride, the sound of their horses fading swiftly into the distance.

Then a voice at the front of the office yelled: 'You still in there Sheriff?' It sounded like Wainwright's voice, but Matt could not be certain.

Hogan answered almost immediately. 'I'm here, Wainwright. What's on your mind?'

'We've come to take Turner. Don't try to stop us, Slim. We mean to have him before his pals come to take him out.'

A pause, then he heard the outer door open and Hogan's voice, hard and authoritative, said: 'Better disperse and go home, men. I don't want to have to shoot any of you, but you're breaking the law doing this. Turner is locked up in jail and he ain't going no place.'

'Better step aside, Slim.' Menace in Wainwright's voice now, deliberate and calculated. 'You ain't going to stop us this time. Me and the boys have been talking things over in the saloons and we've decided — '

'You've decided.' There was a scathing anger in Hogan's voice now. 'I make the decisions around this town, Chet. Since when have you been elected sheriff of Saddlerock?'

'We don't like the way you're shielding that killer in there. You needn't think there's anythin' personal in this, Slim, but we mean to take him and stretch his neck on a rope.'

Hogan's tone was cold as he said: 'The first man to set foot inside here is likely to get his head blown off. You can be the first if you like, Wainwright.'

There was a long silence at that. Very faintly, Matt heard the muttering of the men with Wainwright. Then the other said loudly: 'All right, boys, let's leave him with the sheriff for the night. Reckon we can wait until morning. But we'll be back then, Sheriff, and you'd better not stand in our way then, or we'll come in shooting. No use getting yourself shot up just to protect a killer like that.'

There was the sound of men moving

away back along the street to the saloon, then silence.

* * *

Shivering a little as the cold night air blew through the window of the cell, Matt sank down on to the bunk. Whether those men would carry out their threat in the morning, he did not know for sure, but they had sounded mighty confident of themselves. He doubted if the sheriff would be able to hold them off for long. Sooner or later he would be forced to leave the jail and then the others would take their chance and get him. Once he was in their hands, he doubted if Hogan would be able to do anything even if he should want to.

After all, as far as the sheriff was concerned, he was the man who had shot down his brother and that would be a sufficient excuse to want him dead. So long as a semblance of law and order was maintained, that was all

Sheriff Hogan was worried about; he felt sure on that point.

A few moments later there was the sound of the door at the end of the passage opening and he heard the slow approach of someone moving towards the cell. Then he caught a faint glimpse of the dark figure of the sheriff, standing just outside the cell door.

With an effort he forced himself to his feet. There was a dull ringing in his head and the place seemed to be tilting crazily around him as the blood rushed pounding across his temples.

'You still awake, Turner?' The other's voice reached him softly from just beyond the door.

'Sure, I'm awake. You got something on your mind, Sheriff? Or maybe you think you can finish me before the others come back in the morning.'

'Reckon you ought to know me better than that.' A pause, then the other went on: 'I've been thinking things over about you, Turner. The more I think about this, the more convinced I am you're not guilty of this charge.'

'Well, thanks, but that doesn't help me overmuch with that mob screaming for my blood in the morning.'

'Mebbe it does. Seems to me that nobody but a fool would pull a trick like holding up the stage, relievin' it of a hundred thousand dollars' worth of gold, and then come riding boldly back into town as you did. Not unless he had a pretty good reason and I can't figure one for you.'

'Like I told you before, Sheriff, I didn't hold up that stage and I didn't kill your brother, or anyone else. I've been in Tucson, and although I don't know whether I can prove that or not, it's the truth.'

'I believe you and I'm going to give you a chance to prove your innocence.'

'How?' Matt moved forward a little and peered at the other through the bars of the cell.

'I'm taking a big chance on you, Turner, because I feel that you're not one of those men and because if I keep you here they'll string you up in the morning like they threatened, and knowing the feeling in this town about what happened, I'm not sure I could stop 'em.'

'What do you intend to do?' Matt felt a sudden rising of hope in his body.

'I'm turning you loose right now. You'll get your guns back and I'll bring your mount around to the back of the building. From then on you'll be on your own. Either you run and keep on running, or you'll do what I think you'll do and try find those varmints who framed you with this murder and robbery charge.'

'What makes you think I can ever hope to track 'em down if you and your posse have failed?'

The sheriff shrugged his shoulders. 'Like me, you got a good cause to get 'em. They killed my brother — they want to see you strung up and they've done everything they can to do that.' He said nothing further but moved back along the passage. When he came back a few minutes later he had Matt's guns with him. Opening the cell door he thrust them at him, said tightly: 'Your horse is out back, ready saddled. The townsfolk are at the saloon still talking things over, I reckon. You'd better ride out — and fast — if you want to get out of Saddlerock alive.'

Matt drew in a deep breath and then let the air out in small pinches. He thrust the guns deep into their holsters, felt a little better now that he was armed, then followed the sheriff softly along the passage and out through the door at the far end. The cold night air caught him and wiped some of the tension from his body. In the distance, further along the street, there was still a racket coming from the direction of the saloon. Swinging up into the saddle, he edged the horse out of the narrow alley into the main street.

3

Owlhoot Trail

Even as he rode out into the open, a man yelled, full and long, from somewhere along the street. Almost immediately afterward a gun shouted and then there were more yells. Dimly, as he crouched forward over the neck of his mount, Matt heard Wainwright's voice, harsh and tense, lifted above the others.

'There goes that killer, Turner, boys. Get after him.'

There was a rush from down the street. A gun barked twice, the stilleto stabs of flame lancing through the darkness. Matt felt something invisible tug at the brim of his hat and something fanned his cheek before whining away into the night. As though these shots had been a signal, others broke out from the boardwalk and windows, from right and left and straight behind him. He knew he stood no chance as long as they could see him and that he had to get out of town and along that trail which led up into the hills. Somehow, he had to throw them off and in a hurry. Already there came the thunder of spurred horses at his back as the men mounted up, determined that he should not get out of town alive. As yet nobody seemed to have voiced their thoughts as to how he had broken out of the jail. He wondered for a second, with a part of his mind, just how Slim Hogan was going to explain things away once they got around to asking him questions.

But that was for the other to think out and he put the thought out of his mind almost at once. A fusillade of shots broke out in front of him and the horse reared suddenly as a nickle-tipped bullet scoured across his chest, reared in the middle of a deadly shaft of light that spilled from one of the buildings on his left. Savagely he slashed downward with the rowels of his spurs, felt them dig into the horse's flanks. It dropped its hooves sharply, then pounded forward as more slugs tore through the spot where he had been a moment before. He sucked air down into his heaving lungs, continued to press his body tightly down against the horse's neck to present a more difficult target. In front he saw the small group of men who had been alerted by the shouting and firing, and who had now run out into the middle of the street, clearly in an attempt to block his path and stop him from leaving town, while the others came up on him from behind. His gun was out in his right hand now, his thumb on the hammer, pulling it back. He fired twice at a flash that came from the middle of the street, saw the man suddenly pitch sideways, clutching at a torn shoulder, dropping his gun into the dust at his feet as he sagged to his knees.

Straight out of the yellow shaft of

light, straight towards that line of men he rode, knowing that he had no chance unless he put the horse right at them and scattered them from his path. The men at his back would be coming up on him fast now, and he had to increase his lead somehow, otherwise they would catch up with him within minutes. They must know this country like the back of their hands and he would stand little chance in the darkness unless he managed to keep well ahead of them.

The men in front of him broke when he was yet ten yards from them, the horse thudding down on them from the middle of the street. He felt a grim sense of satisfaction in his mind as he charged through their midst and rode out into the darkness which lay beyond. He dimly heard a man's high-pitched scream as the flailing hooves of the horse caught him and hurled him to one side, sending him down. Then he was through, thundering towards the edge of town, and now there was no more light ahead of him, he was riding swiftly into total darkness.

He gave a quick look behind him, saw the dark shapes of the men riding on his tail, touched the nervous animal's sides again with the spurs, felt the horse respond gallantly to the effort required of it, hooves pounding on the dirt of the street. Then he was out of the town; for a second there was the hollow rattle of hooves over the wooden planks of the bridge, then the thud on the rocky trail that led north half a mile further on, rising into the hill country.

He wondered vaguely how far his pursuers would follow him in that direction. In the dark, without the sheriff to lead them, perhaps not very far. If they really thought the outlaw gang was hidden out somewhere in that direction, they might pause to think twice about following him far.

The thought prompted him to head north as he reached the intersection in the trail. Behind him the noise of pursuit still continued, and he felt a strange tightening in his chest as gunshots rang out, indicating that he might still be within range of their weapons.

He stayed with the main upward trail for perhaps a mile, ears listening keenly for the sounds behind him, trying to judge just where the main body of men lay. They still seemed to be clinging to his trail and any hope he might have had that they would give up the pursuit once it became apparent that he was headed for the hills was soon lost. Gritting his teeth, acutely aware of the ache in his body, he leaned further forward in the saddle. The flanks of his mount soon began to heave with the effect of the punishing pace as the strain began to tell on it. It would have been far better if the sheriff had managed to get a fresh horse for him. His own mount had been tired by that long ride through the alkali and there had been little chance for it to rest up properly.

Gradually he was aware that a small bunch of men must have broken away from the main group and were swinging a little to the west of him, heading hard across country to cut him off before he reached the comparative shelter of the hills. He lifted his head a little, tried to trace their position, but with the confusing thunder of hooves at his back sending the echoes through the night darkness, it was impossible to estimate exactly where they were or where they intended to swing in again in an attempt to box him in between the two groups.

These men knew this part of the territory intimately. He could never hope to throw them off his trail completely so long as he was out in the open. Once among the rocks and timber belt he stood a far better chance, but that still lay several miles ahead, and if he knew anything of the men who rode on his heels, they did not intend to give him the chance of getting there.

For perhaps half a mile he managed to keep his lead. But it was soon apparent that his mount was slowing fast, that it was almost at the end of its strength. It was little short of a miracle that it had succeeded in carrying him as far as this in its present condition. Tired after the long haul over the alkali of the past two days, losing blood from the bullet wound in its chest, it had somehow managed to pull out sufficient strength to get him here, but it would not be able to keep it up much longer.

Narrowing his gaze, he probed the darkness that lay in front of him, seeking the first indication that he was approaching pine country. He knew that it lay somewhere in front of him, covering the rising slopes of the hills where they rose up on the northern skyline. But he could see nothing but flat country stretching in front of him, with no cover, no place for him to halt and perhaps hold these men off long enough for his mount to get back its wind.

A little later he crossed a track that swung in from the east, crossed the trail he was taking, and vanished to his left. The horse frequently slowed, breathing hard, flanks heaving. Desperately he urged it on. Behind him he could hear a vague shouting, the echoes of the men behind him a steady and increasing abrasion in the night.

Bullets were coming still, but most of the men at his back were firing wild, shooting off their guns blindly into the night. Now that they were deep into the wilder country, the ground underfoot on the trail was softer than it had been nearer the town and his horse made far less sound than it had there, so that it was correspondingly more difficult for them to track him by ear.

Presently he noticed the faint haze of dust that showed up against the darker background of the night and a little thrill of apprehension went through him as he realised how close that other, smaller bunch was. He had not realised that they could have ridden so far ahead of him. Now they were swinging in quickly. The sound of their approach grew and came down to him on the small wind that had sprung up. Then, almost before he knew it, he was in the notch of a wide canyon that lay sprawled across the trail. His own dust drag would give away his position, he thought tightly, if he halted here and waited for them to come up to him. The rough, rocky walls of the canyon held him tightly to the trail so that it was impossible for him to swing out of it and head in any other direction. He was well boxed in, could only try to outrun the others until he came out of the canyon and into the open again. Shots reached him, made tiny flutters in the still air about him. He had no idea how long the canyon might be, but he urged the flagging horse savagely, digging spurs into flanks, pushing the animal to a brisker pace. The firing at his back stayed brisk, not heavy volleys but short, sharp bursts, interspersed with moments of silence. Halfway up the canyon with still some way to go, he heard the firing die into a silence that was made deeper and more intense by the racket that had gone before. Then he caught the on-travelling murmur of horses, still close on his heels and getting nearer.

He was still trapped in the walls of the canyon. The horse jumped into a dispirited run as he jabbed spurs into it once more. Its shoes struck hard on the rocky floor of the canyon. Then the tall walls of sandstone began to drop about him. Moments later he came out into the open, spurred his mount off the trail, heading to the east.

Looking anxiously over his shoulder, he caught the cloud dust of the main body of men as it burst clear of the canyon. A sigh of relief escaped from his lips as the realisation came to him that they had missed his move entirely, were still heading along the trail to the north, expecting him to continue his break for the hills, which were his only sanctuary in that area.

Deliberately he slowed his mount's pace. By the time the men discovered their mistake he hoped to be well away into the rough country that lay ahead of him. It still wanted more than four hours to dawn and the moon that lay low on the eastern horizon gave very little light.

He had been riding for less than a quarter of an hour when he realised that although the main body of his pursuers had missed him, there were still men on his trail. Seconds fled as he swivelled in the saddle, tried to pick them out with his eyes, then saw them coming up fast, a little to one side of him but close enough to mean trouble. The realisation came to him that this had to be that small splinter group which had broken away from the main body in an attempt to cut him off. Either they had spotted his move or, more likely, they had been ordered to follow this trail on the chance he might try something like this.

Too far yet for him to be able to judge how many there were, he knew that with his mount in its present tired condition, he could never hope to outrun them. He would have to stop and try to pick them off. The road in front of him passed through a narrow belt of tumbled rock and then a fringe of timber that stood at the back of the line of boulders.

Urging his mount forward, he put it through the boulders, felt it slip and slide under him on the treacherous surface before it gained the other side. Then he reined the horse, slid from the saddle and pulled the Winchester from its scabbard. Throwing himself down in the tangled underbrush, he lay flat on his stomach, peering into the moonlit darkness. He could just pick out the small band of men riding towards the trees, saw them begin to slow as if they had divined his intention and were being doubly cautious now there was the distinct possibility of an ambush having been set for them.

Perhaps three dozen yards away from where he lay, the small knot of riders stopped, sat their mounts quite still, as if listening. Soon they would be satisfied that he had stopped somewhere and then they would begin to spread out and move in to take him from all sides.

Grimly he sighted the rifle on them, determined not to give them that opportunity. He took careful aim, then quickly squeezed the trigger, felt the weapon buck against his shoulder and heard the sharp report in his ears a moment before one of the men pitched out of the saddle and lay still. He did not want to fight and kill these men. As far as he knew, they were all decent citizens of Saddlerock, brought to this pitch of fighting frenzy by a handful of men who wanted to see him killed, who believed, possibly quite sincerely, that he had been connected with that stage robbery in which three deputies and the driver had been shot down in cold blood.

Hidden by darkness and the thick undergrowth, he was able to fire again without any of the return fire coming anywhere near him. The men scattered and he heard one of them yell some orders, saw them pull their mounts back out of range and then drop to the ground, running forward with their guns gleaming faintly in the moonlight.

Swiftly Matt swung, fired at a running shadow, saw it melt into the rocks and was not sure whether he had hit the man or not. There had been no way of telling from the manner in which he had gone to ground.

A bullet broke ground ahead of him and he knew that the muzzle fire of his Winchester must have given away his position to the others. Two more slugs splintered chips of bark from a nearby tree as he jumped to one side, edging back towards his mount. Lead came through the undergrowth in harsh, gusty snorts and crashed into the lower branches just over his head as he kept it low, moving doubled over. Matt backed away still further, moving deeper into the thick timber. He had done what he had set out to do; drawn the men well away from their mounts. Catching the horse by the bridle, he stood absolutely still, fast-thinking, searching intently with eyes and ears.

The firing had ceased for a moment. The marksmen would be taking time off to reload, to possibly try to improve their position and meanwhile, if he stayed here much longer there was the very definite chance that they might be able to swing round and cut off his trail to his rear, in spite of everything he could do to pin them down, or a chance shot might sooner or later reach him or cripple his mount.

He paused for a moment near a thick clump of mesquite, tried to make out the position of the men, found that his field of vision was too limited to see them all now that they had begun to spread out in a wide semi-circle, moving in slowly and purposefully from the horns of the line. Ducking back, he caught the horse, pulled it out from the tall trees to where a thin, winding trail ran through the timber. A volley crashed out at that same instant.

The hum of lead through the trees sounded in his ears like a flight of angry hornets passing close to him. Catching the reins in his left hand, he thrust the long-barrelled Winchester back into its scabbard, slipped the horse out of the brush and went up swiftly into the saddle. Taking care to make no sound, he edged the mount more than thirty feet through the trees, bending low as thorny branches whipped savagely at his unprotected face, before the party's fire began to swing around and follow him, reaching at his back as he increased the gait of the horse.

He veered in and out of the trees, letting the horse pick its own forward gait now, trusting it instinctively, knowing that its senses in the pitch blackness were far better than his own. A bullet scuttled along the trail and whined past him in murderous ricochet, but that was all.

Swiftly now he ran along the winding trail as the trees on either side thinned.

Turning with the trail's gradual curve he came out of the trees a few moments later, glanced back over his shoulder and saw that he was still sheltered from his pursuers. For a fraction of a second he paused in the saddle and studied his situation, looking intently about him in all directions. The timber made a long line of thick shadow across the country, with a rough but passable slope directly in front of him.

He knew that for a little while at least those men would be wary and doubly cautious, not wanting to move in too close for fear of being picked off by a rifle bullet, but once they were sure that he had fled, that he was no longer there in the timber, they would continue to come after him. Rifle fire still sounded in the distance as he put spurs to his mount. Riding over another short passable vista, he pushed forward into the darkness, and in this manner he worked himself a couple of miles towards the distant hills with still no sign of pursuit behind him.

A little later he was forced to fight his way over some of the roughest ground he had ever encountered; forced to dismount at intervals and lead the horse as tangling vine undergrowth over slippery, treacherous rocks circled huge masses of stone. That was the way of it for almost half an hour. At the end of that time, the ground grew more open and he rode easily in the saddle, eyes alert, keeping well balanced to make it easier on the tired horse.

He felt reasonably confident now that he had thrown off the others from his trail, but he did not stop to make camp even though every nerve and muscle in his body ached intolerably and he knew that his mount was almost at the end of its tether. In front of him lay the hills, reaching for perhaps two hundred and fifty miles, giving shelter to all of the lawless element in that neck of the woods. Somewhere in there, he felt certain, were the men who had gone to so much trouble to frame him, who had succeeded in turning him into a wanted man; a killer.

He felt the anger rising inside him again at that thought, and knew that Sheriff Hogan had been right in one respect; he would not rest until he had tracked down and destroyed, or brought in for trial, every last member of that outlaw gang.

But first he had to discover their identity and that could be a truly tricky and difficult business.

★ ★ ★

Daybreak showed the tall spiking summits of the hills outlined against the greying sky. Matt Turner reined his mount at the foot of the rough trail that wound up among the rocks on the low slopes, forcing himself to remain awake. He had ridden throughout the whole of the long night, and now he had reached the hills. He knew with a deep instinct that the men from Saddlerock would not follow him now. This was the land for the lawless.

He stayed with the main trail upward and presently it took him out on to a wide plateau of ground, studded here and there with mesquite and thorn. The trail still continued upward at this point, but he halted, swung down from the saddle cautiously. There was the faint but unmistakable smell of wood smoke in the air, coming from somewhere close at hand. Hefting the Colt into his right, he stepped towards the brush that grew thick and tangled on the very edge of the plateau some twenty yards away.

There he saw nothing but he knew that somewhere around one corner or another of this place men stood and possibly knew of his approach. He took it carefully and slow, ready for the slightest movement, keeping himself on the balls of his feet, ready to move in any direction. A moment later, edging through the brush, he came upon the camp fire in the middle of the small clearing. His tension sharpened as he saw there was no one there, although the frying pan beside the fire was full of bacon and there was a blackened coffee pot near it with the steam still rising from it. The feel of danger lay in him like a tangible thing and he eased himself out into the open with the gun still in his hand, now swinging round to cover the thick bushes which lay all about him. In a slow and easy tone, he said, thrusting the Colt back into its holster.

'All right. Come on out.'

For a moment nothing happened. Then he heard the rustle of the bushes at his back and turned slowly to face the two men who strode out into the clearing. One carried a rifle in his hands and the barrel was trained on him. The other, a younger man, had a narrow, pinched face and close-set, shifty eyes that ran a quick look over Matt, taking in everything. They both had the look of the hunted about them, Matt decided. He did not recognise either man and guessed that he was safe enough to put his plan into operation, a plan that had been forming slowly through the long hours of the night he had ridden north.

After considering Matt closely for a long moment, the man with the rifle lowered the weapon, although he still kept a tight grip on it. Suspicion lay on his broad features.

'Never seen you in these parts before,' he said tightly. 'Where you from?'

'Saddlerock.' Matt spoke easily, noticed the flare of brightness in the man's eyes and the sudden hardening of his face. 'Pulled a job there a couple of days ago. Bunch of us. Held up the stage with the bullion.'

The other man said: 'You riding with Chapman then?' He nodded, motioned towards the fire. 'Help yourself to the bacon and coffee. We got plenty here and you look as if you've been riding hard all night. A posse on your trail?'

Matt squatted at the fire, stretched

his legs out in front of him to ease the dull ache and the shooting fingers of cramp in the big muscles of his thighs. He shook his head emphatically. 'Not any longer. They followed me part of the way outa town, then I lost 'em some miles back. Reckon they won't want to ride here to get me.'

The tall, bearded man laughed harshly, set the rifle down against an upthrusting rock beside him. 'They know better,' he said grimly. 'Ain't been no sheriff or marshal set foot in these hills since we shot Boone a coupla years back.'

Matt teased the bacon with his knife, chewed on it gratefully. For the first time he realised just how hungry he was. The long ride, keeping one jump ahead of that lynch mob, had taken more out of him than he had realised. As he sat there eating the hot bacon and washing it down with the scalding coffee, a riot of thoughts continued to spill through his whirling mind. He had not expected things to go quite as simply as that. Perhaps he ought to have guessed the identity of that gang before now, he told himself fiercely. Chapman and his two brothers and possibly riding with Clayburn, one of the worst killers this side of the border. It was the kind of robbery they specialised in and they alone would have a motive for wanting him convicted and hanged for murder.

Since he had testified against them and got them long jail sentences for their part in a hold-up, there had always been the chance they might bust out of jail and come looking for him. This way they had almost succeeded in killing two birds with one shot. Getting away with a hundred thousand dollars' worth of gold bullion and effectively putting the blame on him.

'My name's Gilpin,' said the bearded man harshly. 'This is my brother Jed.' He lifted bushy, black brows. 'Something happen in Saddlerock?'

'Why do you figger that?' Matt looked directly at him, holding the long-bladed knife balanced in his right hand.

The other shrugged. He evidently had decided to treat Matt with a little more respect now that he had heard the other was a member of one of the most notorious outlaw bands in the country. 'Guessed you wouldn't ride back into Saddlerock after taking all of that gold, without a good reason. A man would be a fool to do that.'

Matt gave a brief nod, finished his meal and wiped the plate clean with sand, then drained his mug of coffee.

A glinting expression showed on the other's face. 'They still lookin' for yuh?'

'That's right. Somebody had to ride back and check on things. I wasn't known there, so I went.'

'Where are the rest of the boys hidin' out?' asked the younger man. 'Could be that me and Clint might join up with you. We can handle guns as well as the next man and we've had some experience.'

'That'd be up to Chapman. I'd have

to see him first. They said they'd be along this slope of the hills, but I ain't seen no sign of 'em so far. When I smelled the smoke from your fire, I had you figgered for 'em. That's why I wasn't too concerned about you. Seems they must be further than I reckoned.'

Jed shook his head. 'We been here a week or so now. We ain't seen anybody pass. If they did, they'll be well inside the hills by now. It'll be another day's ride for you at least.'

Matt sensed a certain nervousness in these two men, guessed they had been too long on the run from the law, knew that even here in the hills their luck could some day run out if they didn't manage to join up with one of the big outfits operating here. He turned over the information they had given him in his mind. Now he knew far more than he had just a little while before. He knew the faces and names of the men he was seeking and he had a rough idea where they might be found.

'Understand now,' broke in Jed

quickly. 'We don't want to go horning our way in on a man like Chapman, but reckon he can always do with a couple of extra guns.'

'Could be he might at that,' mused Matt, thinking fast. 'You figgerin' on staying around these parts for a while?'

'Hell — yes!' grunted the other sourly. He glanced at his brother, then heaved himself heavily to his feet and stood beside the fire. 'Reckon there ain't no place for us to go.' He eyed Matt speculatively. 'You look plain tuckered out, mister. Reckon you might rest up a spell here. Go on after the heat of the day is out. It's going to be another hot day by the look of things.'

Matt glanced up quickly at the brightening sky, nodded, clamping his lips together into a tight line. 'Thanks all the same but I figure I'd better be moving on. They'll be waiting for me in the hills. I'll sure pass on your proposition to Chapman though. If he agrees we'll ride back this way.'

He pushed himself upright, saw the

tall bearded man grip the rifle butt a little more tightly, as if having second thoughts about the whole thing. For a second, danger seemed to hang in the air. Then the other relaxed his grip, let go of the weapon and speared a piece of bacon on the tip of his knife, thrusting it into his mouth chewing slowly.

Matt let his breath go slowly. He glanced across at Jed. 'Thanks for the breakfast. It sure came in welcome.'

He saw the other's quick nod, then moved out of the clearing, back to where he had left his mount. The sorrel was still standing where he had left it, grazing on the lush green grass. It pricked up its ears at his approach. Tightening the cinch a notch, he swung up into the saddle, threw a quick glance back towards the bushes that skirted the clearing, saw the younger man standing there watching him closely. Lifting his hand, he wheeled his mount and set it up along the trail that wound around the summit of the hills towards the pass where the other trail edged its way up the steep slope.

He rode deliberately slowly, feeling the weariness in his bones begin to take a tighter hold of him. He had the feeling that the two men he had just left, particularly the black-bearded one, did not fully believe his story. It was highly likely they would make an attempt to follow him, either to allay their suspicions, or to get him to lead them to Chapman. Either way, it was essential that he should shake them off. Once he met up with the Chapman gang, he did not want another group of outlaws at his back when it came to the showdown. There was no doubting what the actions of the Gilpin brothers would be if he tried to shoot it out with Chapman and his men. This would be the opportunity those two would need to get themselves into favour with Chapman.

The sun came up, literally bounding up from beyond the horizon and very soon the heat of the day began to make itself felt. He tipped the broad-brimmed hat on to the back of his head, lifted it off at intervals to wipe the sweat band with his bandana. As he rode he looked at the sun-glaring hills which lay all about him, eyeing the solidness of them. In a way it helped him, that feel of solidity all around him, gave him something on which to fix his thoughts. That was the funny thing about all of this, he mused. In the old days not so long ago, he had ridden the range with scarcely anything to worry him, completely and utterly carefree. There were few cares and everything was fun, and then it had been an easy thing to smile. The past had meant nothing to him in those days and the future was something which had yet to come.

Now all of that seemed to have become finished almost overnight, it seemed. The only thing which claimed his mind was to keep one step ahead of the law and to track down those men who had framed him with this charge, the men who had tried their best to destroy him completely. The thought hurried him, crowded in on him, and left little room in his mind for anything else. With an effort he tried to reach out with his mind to the days before all of this had happened, staring at the tall canyons that opened out in front and on either side of him, but not really seeing the deep red sandstone, the sharp shadows which slashed blackly across them, places where the sunlight never seemed to reach. His forehead was furrowed with deep lines of concentration, his long rugged face showing the intensity of his thoughts.

But he could remember very little. It was as if those thoughts, those memories, refused to come back to him, were to be forever forgotten, locked away in his mind where he was unable to get at them. He no longer felt free. The trails were no longer open to him. At every turn, in every town he came to, he would be a marked man. There would be the wanted posters pasted up at every turn, warning people to be on the look out for him, offering a reward for his capture, dead or alive. There might even be bounty hunters after his scalp at that very moment, hoping to claim the reward for his capture. Quite suddenly he felt all burnt out and useless. It was as if part of his brain told him quite clearly that it would never be possible for him to return to the old days unless he succeeded in clearing his name. He wasn't the same man who had ridden out of Saddlerock only a few days earlier, bound for Tucson. It was a different man who rode along that narrow, twisting hill trail, seeking men he had decided to kill.

Quite suddenly, he realised that he had been riding almost half asleep in the saddle, swaying back and forth, not paying any attention to what was going on around him. He reined his mount at a sharp bend in the trail, straigtened up and forced himself to listen intently. At first he heard nothing but the call of some bird in the stunted bushes close at hand. Then, quite clearly and unmistakably, he picked out the faint and faraway sound of hooves on the trail some distance behind him. He twisted his lips into a grim smile, nodding slowly to himself. The Gilpin brothers still on his trail, still following him at a distance so as not to arouse his suspicions.

He let them come after him for a while, then pulled off the trail into a narrow belt of trees, making camp in the shade. The smell of the pines was sharp and aromatic in his nostrils, a welcome relief to the acrid stench of dust on the trail itself. Throwing himself down on the tough, springy grass, he built himself a smoke and stretched himself out in the shade of the trees. Along the trail a piece, the sound of the approaching riders faded. He knew they had guessed his action, and would not come any closer until he moved out again. Promptly he forgot their presence, drew the smoke from the cigarette deep into his lungs and let the warmth soak into his tired body.

He woke when the sun threw its glare on to his face and knew that he had been asleep for several hours. The sun was past its zenith, lowering to the west and the shadows were beginning to lengthen. He got to his feet and stretched his limbs. He felt better after the rest, but there was a dry taste in his mouth, and he drunk the last of the water from his canteen, swilling it around his mouth for several seconds before letting it slide down his throat.

Still no sound from along the trail. The men behind him would be taking the opportunity to rest during the heat of the noon but he guessed one of them would have remained awake, listening for him to start his ride again. Just how dangerous those two men were, he wasn't sure. He had no real reason for killing either of them, but he knew deep within himself that he would do so if the act was forced upon him by circumstances. He had changed in a great many ways during the past few days. Now he was a man fighting for his existence, determined to prove his innocence or die in the attempt.

He swung up into the saddle, moved the horse out of the shade and onto the trail, letting it pick its way forward slowly, making scarcely any sound. Not that this would throw those two off the trail, he reflected. They would start to ride after him once more as soon as the darkness fell, whether they heard him move out or not.

Around him now everything was quiet and still, an ominous stillness that began to eat like acid at his nerves. The smell of the day as it began to slowly die was compounded of bitter-strong dust and harsh, burnt grass. Shortly before nightfall he reached the pass and moved through it, with the rocky walls rising high above him on either side, blotting out the last red rays of the setting sun. As he came out on the other side, began to ride down into the undulating country that lay here in the middle of the hills, the sun dropped swiftly below the western horizon in a sudden brilliant burst of flame, tinging the clouds that lay along the skyline with scarlet. But even this faded swiftly as the short twilight darkened and then the night came stealing in swiftly from the east, throwing a deep purple and then a black haze over everything. The air was cold now, with a breeze blowing down the face of the higher slopes, and he felt it brush his face, easing the burning touch of the sun.

He threw off a couple of ridges before full darkness, then made camp a little way from the trail, not building a fire but content to lie in his blanket in the cool darkness, ears alert for all of the little sounds of the night, his brain interpreting them all, telling him which could spell danger and which were innocuous. When he heard the run of horses further down the trail, he crushed out the glowing tip of his smoke and sat on his haunches, the guns in his hands, waiting. He listened to the horses come on. They were moving at a fast pace and he doubted if this was Jed Gilpin and his brother following on his heels. It was not likely they would give their presence away in that manner. Whoever it was riding hell for leather in the darkness, they were completely unaware of his presence there, although it was possible that his dust wake might warn them another rider had passed along the trail only a short time before.

Sound and riders came quickly around the bend in the trail a quarter of a mile from his camp. He heard someone give a harsh shout, then saw the small knot of men as they rode swiftly past the spot, the drumming of their horses' hooves making a fading abrasion in the night. It had been impossible to recognise any of the men. They were obviously in a hurry to get some place and the thought came to him that it might have been the Chapman gang. For a moment he crouched there in the stillness, undecided whether or not to follow them.

Then he decided against it. In the darkness, if he came upon the Chapman band without warning, it might be the worse for him, particularly with the Gilpin brothers still so close on the trail.

With no fire, he slept cold that night, woke shivering as the dawn was streaking the horizon with grey. Rolling out of the blanket, he rolled himself another smoke, but it tasted sharp and bitter on his tongue, reminding him that he had neither food nor water now.

He waited until the dawn had brightened, then saddled up, rode along the twisting trail which the riders of the previous night had taken. A couple of miles further on he came suddenly upon the small clearing. In the centre of it a small cluster of huts had been erected. He paused and sat quite still, taking it all in for several moments before he realised what it was. At some time or other in the past men had come up here, digging in the rocks for gold. There was an axe, still buried deep in the trunk of one of the trees in the clearing, the handle protruding at an angle from the wood, the head dulled now by long exposure to the elements.

Very slowly and carefully he eased himself from the saddle. In the ground ahead of him he was able to make out the prints which indicated that riders had been here and recently. Jerking one of the Colts from his holster, he moved out cautiously into the open. This seemed just the kind of place where the Chapman gang might hide out until the heat was off and they could make their way into one of the towns to get rid of their loot. Slitting his eyes against the glare of the sunlight, he cast about him for any sign of horses, but could see none. No sound came from any of the old buildings as he edged forward. Reaching the first, he scouted around it, then pushed open the door with his foot, moving inside quickly, stepping sharply to one side as he entered, expecting to hear the bark of a gun and feel the slam of lead striking him. But the hut was empty. There were the remains of bunks around the walls and dust on the floor, virgin dust with no marks in it to indicate that it had been disturbed in any way for years. He relaxed a little. Certainly no one had used this place for a long time, but there were indications that one of the other buildings had been used. He noticed a pile of empty bean cans outside one of the huts, the metal still shiny, knew that they had not been there for long.

Pressing his body tightly against the wall of the hut, he put his ear to the wood and listened. There was no sound inside. Finally he kicked the door open and threw himself inside, taking no chances. Here again the hut was empty, but on the floor by the long, wooden table there were a couple of empty saddlebags. There was also the shattered remains of a strongbox which had been kicked out of the way into the corner of the room. On the table he found the remains of a meal with a stack of dirty dishes.

Carefully he went around the place, checking on everything he found. At the end of that time he was convinced that the Chapman gang had been here, but that he was too late. They had pulled out, possibly they might even have split up for the time being, going on the belief that in ones and twos they could escape detection far more easily. They would have to get rid of the gold in some way but he didn't doubt that they would know of someone who would pay them well for it.

He went back outside, stared up at the bright heavens, sucking air down into his lungs. If the gang had split up, it was going to be more difficult than ever to track them down.

4

Ride the High Hills

By high noon the heat had grown in savage intensity and there was a dull throbbing at the back of Matt's eyes as he swung along the western trail which would eventually lead him down from the hills and out on the trail into Tucson. If the Chapman gang had split up, the odds were that at least one of them would head for Tucson. He needed to catch up with only one of them to make him talk and tell him where the others were. The thought sent a grim feeling of pleasure through him and involuntarily he tightened his grip on the leather of the reins, his right hand resting just a few inches above the handle of the Colt at his waist. He had found some food in the abandoned hut and had eaten for the first time since he had left the Gilpin's camp. Now his belly was growling contentedly as he sat tall in the saddle, watchful and alert.

By and by the country over which he rode roughened. He was on the downgrade slopes of the hills now, back among the tumbled rocks and boulders which littered the trail at every turn. It was soon apparent that this trail was not used as often as that by which he had ridden up into the hills. He held to the crests of the ridges for as long as possible, pausing at intervals to scan the ground below him. From his vantage point up there, it was possible for him to see for miles, down where the valley opened out at the base of the hills, his vision now limited only by the shimmering heat haze which successfully obscured most of the further details.

By mid-afternoon he had reached the head of the main trail and was on the point of urging the horse downward when his keen gaze spotted the cloud of dust-smoke in the distance down on the flat floor of the valley. Narrowing his gaze, he managed to pick out the dim shape of the rider, spurring his mount cruelly into the distance, and a sudden conviction gripped him and he knew, almost without thinking, that the man down there spurring his mount at such a punishing pace was one of the Chapman gang, one of the men he was hunting.

He put his mount to the downgrade trail, raking spurs along its flanks. Fortunately, the sorrel was a sure-footed beast and had rested well during the night, and they made good time, reaching the valley floor half an hour later, the dust trail standing out behind them, outlined against the grey and red of the rocks. He wondered briefly whether the rider had turned and spotted the trail at his back, but the thought was swiftly pushed into the background of his mind as the sorrel gallantly lengthened its stride. It took him another half hour to bring the rider into sight again. The man was moving at an angle to the trail, not heading for

Tucson directly but by a roundabout route. Matt speculated on this as he rode, but could find no answer to it, knew only that the other would have to camp some time and that he might be able to take him then when the man did not expect trouble.

At a swiftly flowing creek he paused to let his mount drink and blow, filling his canteen with the cold, clear water and slaking his own thirst. Then he mounted up again and continued the pursuit. By nightfall he felt sure that the other was now only a little way ahead of him and he slowed the pace of the sorrel, listening for any sound that might give away the other rider's position. When he realised that he could no longer hear the hoofbeats of the other's mount, he felt a faint twinge of uncertainty. It was dark now and he could not see very far. Whatever happened, he did not want to blunder on the other without warning. He knew of the reputation of these men; killers who were fast on the draw, men who lived by the gun and who lived only so long as they were able to outdraw their enemies. That was how the members of this gang had stayed alive for so long, and he knew he was up against fast gunslicks who could part a man's hair with a slug at a hundred paces.

He rode in silence for a quarter of an hour, casting about him carefully. Then, just when he figured that he had lost the other completely, his keen gaze picked out the faint flickering red flare of a fire over to his right. He put his mount steadily in that direction, easing it forward so that it picked its way very slowly, making little sound, its hoof-beats deadened by the soft earth of the valley.

He grew anxious to have this thing over and done with, but he let the reins remain slack, trusting the sorrel and fighting down his urgency. For several moments he could no longer see the fire and knew that he had ridden down into a shallow depression, one of the innumerable small basins in the valley.

The other's camp could not be more than a hundred yards away now, he decided, and slid quietly from the saddle, moving forward on foot, his legs brushing the coarse grass where it grew almost to his knees in places.

Then he climbed the edge of the depression, parted some bushes at the top and found himself looking down on to the flickering glow of firelight and saw the man, who sat with his back to him, a dark shadow silhouetted against the fire. It was clear that the other was unaware of his presence there, did not suspect there might be any danger close by. Matt tightened his lips. If this was one of the Chapman gang . . .

The thought tightened every muscle in his body and the knuckles stood out beneath the tight-drawn flesh of his hands as he crouched there. He heard the softly muted whinny of a horse from the shadows on the far side of the camp and tautened abruptly, forcing himself to relax as the man said something in soft tones to the animal.

The other seemed more lax and unconcerned than Matt had thought him to be.

He waited a full two minutes, then eased himself upright, stepped forward a couple of paces until he stood just outside the ring of firelight, the Colt levelled on the other's back. Sharply, he said:

'Just hold it there, mister. Don't try to go for that gun.' He added the last more sharply as the man stiffened and tried to edge his right hand away from in front of him and down towards his gunbelt out of sight of Matt.

The other hesitated, then shrugged and relaxed. He did not turn but said hoarsely: 'What the hell is this? If'n you're trying to hold me up for money, then you got the wrong man, stranger.'

Cautiously, Matt edged around the other until he stood with the fire between them and he could see the man for the first time. His grin widened into a vicious smile and the finger on the trigger of the Colt tightened a little.

'So I was right, after all,' he murmured not once taking his eyes off the other. 'I figured you might try to make it into Tucson once you'd split the loot among you. Where are the other men, Clayburn?'

'Seems to me you know a helluva lot, mister,' snarled the other, eyes bright with hatred and anger. 'Just who are you and what's it to you where anybody is?'

'I guess you don't recognise me, Clayburn,' snapped Matt harshly. His gaze locked hard with the other's. 'Mebbe you and the Chapmans figured I'd have been safely out of the way by now, strung up by the folk in Saddlerock for something I didn't do.'

He saw the look which flashed instantly over the other's hard features and the expression that came into his eyes.

'That's right, Clayburn,' he said throatily. 'I'm Matt Turner, the man you and the others tried to frame with robbery and murder. Trouble is that the sheriff believed my story and now I'm here, and I mean to take the lot of you back with me to stand trial and clear my name.'

The other's lips twisted into a vicious grin. 'If you reckon you're going to take me in alive, then you're mistaken, Turner.' He was still wary but Matt guessed he was just waiting for a chance to go for his guns, waiting for a moment when Matt relaxed his vigilance. 'And if you're mebbe figgerin' that I'm going to talk and tell you where the others are, you're wrong there, too.'

Very slowly Matt shook his head. 'You'll tell me everythin' I want to know before I'm through with you, Clayburn. And if you're figurin' on me not pulling this trigger and sending you straight to hell, you're wrong again. I'd as soon shoot you down in cold blood as kill a rattler. To me you're lower than a snake, so don't push me too far.'

Clayburn deliberately kept his hands in front of him, moving very slowly as he pulled his legs up under him. Not

125

once did his gaze leave Matt's face.

Finally he said thinly: 'Could be that we were wrong about you, Turner. I always had you figured as a smart one, but Chapman didn't reckon so. Now if you was to throw in your hand with us, you'd soon have more money than you knew what to do with and now you've got this rap hanging over your head, you might as well stay with it. Even if you kill me, what good is it going to do you? The others will come riding after you if I don't show up in Tucson and the next time they'll finish the job.'

'That won't help you none,' Matt said decisively. 'I swore I'd hunt down every one of you after they'd thrown me in jail for that stage hold-up and I meant it. Nothing you can say is going to change my mind.'

He stood waiting for the other to make his attempt, to go for his guns. He knew that soon the other would break, was merely waiting for him to relax just a little before he tried to shoot him down. There was a bright glitter in the outlaw's porcine eyes. But the interruption came from a totally different direction.

The harsh voice that rang out from the darkness at Matt's back said hoarsely: 'Better drop that gun, mister. We've been listening to what you've had to say.'

Jed Gilpin's voice. Matt did not have to turn to know that the two brothers would be behind him and that they would have guns trained on him, would back up their threat. He saw the smile of triumph spread slowly over the outlaw's face.

'Reckon you're finished, Turner,' he said gloatingly. He made to get to his feet. 'I don't know who you are out there,' he called, 'but you can come in now. I don't think our friend here will try anythin' stupid and — '

Matt thought fast. He still held his gun on the outlaw, could still pull the trigger and send the other into eternity. But he knew if he did that he would undoubtedly get a bullet in the back.

No doubt that would happen to him anyway. Clayburn would never allow him to live now. They had to make sure he was out of the way for good this time.

He acted instantly as he heard the two men moving up through the grass behind him, hoping that for the moment they were a little off balance, too sure of themselves to act swiftly enough. He saw Clayburn getting to his feet, thrusting his legs under him, his right hand moving with a deceptive slowness for the gun in his belt.

Without thinking, he suddenly hurled himself to one side, dropping back at the same time so that he no longer stood within the light from the fire. His bullet took the outlaw in the chest, sending him staggering back beyond the fire, a dark stain spreading over his shirt. Dead on his feet, the other's eyes began to glaze as he concertinaed to the ground and lay still. For a split second there was no sound after that solitary shot sent the echoes bucketing throught the night.

Then there was the crash of guns at his back as the two outlaws fired blindly in his direction, trying to seek him out. The slugs tore through the air close to his head as he hit the ground with a blow that sent pain hammering along his arm and shoulder. Then he was rolling swiftly to one side, sucking air down into his heaving lungs, twisting on the ground to bring himself face to face with the two men near the camp.

For a long moment his eyes were dazzled by the harsh firelight and he could make out nothing in the darkness through the flickering green haze that persisted in front of his vision. Then he caught a fragmentary glimpse of the shadow that rose up on the edge of the depression and began to edge its way forward. It was impossible from that distance to recognise which of the two brothers it was, but the firelight glinted dully on the revolver in his hand as he crept forward.

He caught sight of Matt at the same

instant as the other spotted him, swung swiftly to bring the gun to bear. Both weapons fired at precisely the same instant. Matt felt the slug burn along the top of his shoulder and he almost dropped the Colt. Through pain-blurred eyes he saw the man pitch forward on to the outer rim of hard, open ground, twitch once or twice and then lie still.

In the deep, intense silence that followed, he tried to discern where the other killer was. It was possible he had crawled around once he had dropped Clayburn, hoping to take him from the rear. That meant he could come from any direction. He cast about him frantically. There was nothing to be seen beyond the circle of firelight. If the other Gilpin was there, he was keeping damnably quiet.

There came a faint rustle in the grass over to his right. He snapped around in that direction, the sweat breaking out on his forehead, his heart pumping madly in his chest. He tried to push himself up on to his feet, gripping the gun tightly in his fist. He could feel the blood beginning to trickle warmly down his flesh, dripping from his wrist.

A gun thundered from somewhere close at hand. The bullet hummed close to his head, whined off into the darkness. He swung round, cursing himself for not watching the right direction. That burst of gunfire had come from some distance to the right of where he had figured the last remaining outlaw to be hiding. He had almost made a fatal mistake. Had that bullet passed an inch to the left it would have drilled him through the head, right between the eyes.

Instinctively, he loosed off a couple of shots into the darkness, ducked as the outlaw fired again. This time the bullet fanned his cheek but scarcely had the bark of gunfire died down than he heard the groan from the darkness, then sound faded and there was only the sharp stink of burnt powder in his nostrils, choking him.

A part of his mind told him that this could be a trick on the other's part. That Gilpin was lying out there, just waiting for him to show himself, when he would put a bullet into him. Then, faintly, he heard the outlaw's guttering, sighing breath, knew that he had been hit. How badly he was not sure. He somehow forced himself to his feet, stood swaying for a long moment, then moved in on the other, waiting to put in the last shot.

Now that he was on his feet he could hear the other twisting and threshing on the ground in obvious pain, but gradually the sounds grew fainter and he ceased eventually to move so that Matt thought he had died, but a moment later the other's voice came to him from the darkness:

'You ain't going to stand a chance against Chapman and the others, stranger. But I hope when they do catch up with you that they kill you slow and hard. I hope they — ' The sound was choked off by a dull rattle, as if the man's breath had suddenly caught in his throat. Matt forced strength into his legs and went forward through the tall grass, over the lip of the depression, until he almost stumbled over the other's body, lying huddled in a small hollow. He bent and touched the outlaw with his good hand, felt the limp slackness of the man's limbs and knew he was dead.

Slowly he stood up, the blood throbbing violently at the back of his eyes. Even now he found it hard to realise that all three outlaws were dead. It had been his own fault that he had walked into that trap, he told himself savagely. He should have remembered that those two men would stick with him, even after he had located that shack in the old mine workings and had then moved off along the other trail.

But the men were dead now and, if he remembered rightly, there would be four others in the gang to account for once he caught up with them and, from what Clayburn had said, they were already in Tucson.

He threw sand on the fire after binding up the wound in his shoulder as best he could, not wishing to be seen before dawn, then stretched himself out on the hard ground, pulled his blanket over him and slept.

It was still dark when he woke but dawn was not far off and he knew it would be dangerous to tarry there in daylight. Saddling up, he managed to pull himself painfully into the saddle and hang on grimly to the reins. His shoulder was stiff and the blood had congealed on it, his shirt sticking to his flesh, irritating and lacerating with every movement he made. He had lost more blood during the night and there was a deep-seated weakness in him now, so that everything about him seemed to swim and sway in front of his vision.

With a supreme effort he forced himself to think clearly. Tucson lay to the east and he turned his mount's head in that direction and began the long ride.

Dawn found him less than three miles from the camp where death had come three times in quick succession. He knew that in his present condition it would be foolish to try to hurry the horse. Even at the pace it was moving, he found it difficult to keep his balance. At times he felt a curious dizziness sweeping over him and there seemed to be little feeling left in his body. When the sun came up it became even worse, even more difficult to remain in the saddle. The heat made the throbbing pain in his temples more difficult to bear and sweat dripped continually into his eyes and he was unable to brush it away. He found himself slipping lower and lower in the saddle, his shoulders hunched forward over the animal's neck. There were long moments when he seemed to be delirious, knew nothing of where he was nor where he was going.

Around him the heat was reflected

back from the smooth, flinty soil of the valley. It shocked even through closed lids, glaring redly into his brain. The wound in his shoulder had opened once more and he could feel the warm stickiness of fresh blood trickling down his chest, soaking into his shirt. His lips were parched and cracked and the water he took into his mouth from his canteen brought no refreshment. His mouth seemed to absorb it as rapidly as he sipped it, his tongue swollen to twice its normal size.

It was close on midday when he noticed the ranch house in the distance, almost directly ahead of him. It was impossible for him to gauge its distance, but somehow he managed to direct the sorrel towards it. Thoughts were scarcely coherent in his mind now. His brain seemed to be continually slipping off into other scenes from the past, scenes which now appeared to have more reality for him than the country through which he was travelling.

The smoothly swaying gait of the sorrel seemed to be an integral part of him now. Blinking his eyes, feeling the grit that had worked its way under the lids scratch and scrape his eyeballs painfully, he tried to focus his gaze on the ranch, opened his mouth to call out for help, but nothing more than a croak escaped from his lips. He could feel his consciousness slipping away from him like a rotten rag and he knew he could not hold on much longer. His body was slipping from the horse and he was unable to control it, to remain upright. The darkness of unconsciousness came rushing at him from all directions, closed over his mind and body in an irresistible wave . . .

★ ★ ★

When Matt finally came round there was the feel of cool sheets against his naked chest and the ceiling over his head looked unfamiliar. For a long moment his mind struggled to orientate itself, his brain trying desperately to remember, to recognise something familiar that could tell him where he was and what had happened. But there was nothing there, his thoughts kept slipping tantalising from him, leaving him with nothing on which to hang.

He tried to push himself up on to his hands, then sank back on to the soft pillow, biting down on the groan that rose unbidden to his lips as pain jarred agonisingly through his right shoulder and down his arm. He lay there for a long moment and forced himself to remember things a little more clearly. He recalled the gun battle at the outlaw's camp in the middle of the valley, some miles away, when he had killed Clayburn and the two Gilpin brothers. He recalled that he had been shot in the shoulder and that he had been trying to make his way into Tucson to locate the other members of the gang. But that was as far as his mind went. After that there was simply a blank and, try as he would, he could not fill it with any concrete details.

He was still lying there when he

heard the door of the room creak open and a second later a girl came into the room and walked over to the bed, staring down at him with a look of concern on her features which rapidly changed to one of satisfaction.

'You're finally awake,' she said in a soft, musical voice. 'I thought you were more badly injured than you really are when I found you.'

He rubbed his forehead with his good hand. 'What happened? Where am I?'

'You're quite safe and in good hands.' She stood beside the bed, smiling down at him. 'I'm Rosaria Lynd. This is my father's ranch. I saw you earlier today, riding in this direction. Before I could get to you, you'd fallen from the horse and it was then I saw you had been shot.'

'How did you get me in here?'

'I dragged you in and got you into bed. It wasn't too far, fortunately.'

'I see.' He lay back and turned the thought over in his mind. He realised that for some reason the girl hadn't queried how he had been shot. He turned his attention from the ceiling over his head and looked back at her. 'I suppose I owe you my life. I was trying to get to Tucson, it's important I should get there as soon as possible. If my shoulder has been bandaged up, I reckon I might be able to — ' He tried to push himself upright again, but the girl thrust him back on to the pillow, firmly and gently.

'I'm afraid you won't be able to leave here for a few days yet. That wound of yours is a little worse than you seem to think. There was some infection in it. I think we've managed to clean it now but it means you won't just be able to saddle up right now and ride on out.'

He sucked in a deep breath, winced a little as a fresh spasm of pain lanced through his shoulder. He eyed the girl carefully. 'You haven't asked me yet how I was shot,' he said tightly. 'For all you know, I could be a killer on the run from the law.'

'I'm quite sure you're not,' she said positively. 'For one thing, you were headed away from the hills, and all of the outlaws in these parts usually go there to get away from the law. And — well, you don't look like a criminal.'

He grinned at that. 'I wonder if you'll still say that when they get around to putting up the wanted posters with my picture on 'em.'

Her brows came together in a delicate line. 'You mean that the law is on your trail?'

'That's right.' He wet his lips, then went on quietly: 'There was a stage hold-up in Saddlerock some days ago. I was in Tucson when it happened, but when I got back into town I found that the gang who'd carried out the hold-up and shot four men in the process had framed me for a part in it. The townsfolk wanted to string me up right away, but Sheriff Hogan believed I was innocent. He let me out of the jail before they could go through with their necktie party, told me that the only way

141

for me to clear my name and prove my innocence was to hunt down that gang and bring them in. I ran one of them to earth last night. Caught up with him in the valley west of here. There were two other polecats on my tail and they butted in at the wrong moment. There was a gunfight and I had to kill them. That was when I got this bullet in me.'

'Yet you say you were riding to Tucson when I found you. Isn't that a foolish thing to do if there are wanted posters out for you?'

'Maybe, but before he died that outlaw told me the other members of the gang were meeting him in Tucson. It's the only lead I've got and I have to follow it through. Now they've got the loot from that stage, they could split up until the turmoil has died down a little and I want to get them before that happens.'

The girl eyed him dubiously. 'You'll only kill yourself if you try to move in your present condition. Two days won't make all that difference.'

'I hope you're right.' He pressed his lips together and tried to go on thinking clearly.

The girl waited for him to go on and when he made no further attempt to speak, said softly: 'Do you really have to go through with this mad idea of trying to bring these four men to justice? You'd be safe here. You could stay as long as you wanted and the law would never touch you.'

'You figure you're big enough to keep the law away? How long do you reckon it would be before somebody came around, visiting maybe, and recognised me from my picture on the posters? Can you stop the Chapman gang from coming and hunting me down?' He shook his head very slowly but definitely. 'They won't rest until they've finished me once they learn I'm still alive and that I've killed Clayburn. You don't know how much they hate me for testifying against 'em some years ago.'

The girl lifted her chin, eyed him steadily and repeated: 'You'd be quite safe here. I promise you that.'

'All right, I believe you, but it can't be. I swore to hunt down those killers and I mean to do it, and there ain't anythin' that's going to stop me.'

The girl sighed. She turned away and walked towards the door. 'I always knew men were stubborn, but I never met one quite like you. I'll make you something to eat.'

She closed the door behind her and Matt lay on the bed with his legs stretched out straight in front him. So long as he lay quite still the pain in his shoulder subsided into a dull ache, diffused throughout his body. Deep within him, he knew that if he had to rest up here for a couple of days, perhaps longer, the Chapmans would grow tired of waiting for Clayburn, and it would not take long for news to filter through into town. Then he would lose the initiative he held at the moment, and the odds would really be stacked against him. Ten minutes later the girl brought a bowl of soup for him.

She was followed by a tall, broad-shouldered man in his early fifties, with iron grey hair and a strangely military bearing.

'My daughter tells me you were shot up by outlaws somewhere to the west, Mister Turner,' he said crisply. 'I'd like to offer you the hospitality of the ranch for as long as you care to stay.'

'That's mighty kind of you, sir.' Matt gave a slight nod. 'I've already explained to your daughter why I have to get into Tucson as soon as possible. This is extremely important.'

The other nodded. 'I understand something of your anxiety, but if you were to ride into town in that state, you'd never make it. Even if you did, you would be in no condition to tackle four outlaws, even if you could find them.'

Matt sighed. 'You're right, of course, and I don't want to sound ungrateful for all you're doing for me.'

He sipped the hot soup slowly, felt it bring some of the warmth and life back into his body. When he had finished the girl took the empty plate and went with it back to the kitchen. Matt could hear her fussing with the plates, then watched as the tall man closed the bedroom door. Coming back into the middle of the room, Lynd said quietly: 'I heard about that stage hold-up in Saddlerock, Turner. I'm also a good friend of Sheriff Hogan's. Seems that you've told the truth, but what you have to know is that he was forced to swear out a warrant for you once Wainwright and the others made it back to town. Seems you shot up a couple of 'em, just wounded 'em, that's all, but they're all firmly convinced now that you were with those outlaws when they held up the stage. There are wanted posters all the way from here to the border by now and plenty in Tucson. If you do intend to go there, then I'd advise you to watch your step or you're likely to be shot down by the law before you get a glimpse of these four men you're looking for.'

'Thanks for the warning,' said Matt softly. 'I've known from the beginning that it isn't going to be easy to get 'em, but if I'm to prove my innocence, then it's the only chance I have.'

'I'd like to help if I can. Everyone in the territory has suffered because of these outlaws.'

Matt shook his head. 'You don't want to be in this quarrel. It's no concern of yours and it could mean a lot of trouble for you.'

'I'm not in it.'

'You will be if they find out how you're shelterin' me and more so if they know you're helping me.'

'Could be you're right, but somebody has to make the first stand against them or they'll end up by running the whole country.'

Matt looked at the other for a moment with a penetrating attention, then forced a quick grin. 'I could have done with a man like you in Saddlerock. It seemed they all thought I'd done it, even when I

147

protested I'd been in Tucson all of the time.'

'When a thing like this happens, people don't act normally and in a rational manner,' said the other gently. 'Four men were shot down in cold blood and they could not forget that. Anger can do strange things to a man. It can turn him from a rational thinking creature into a vicious, snarling animal, and when that happens there's little point in trying to argue with him.'

Conversation touched on various things, moving aimlessly between them after that. Presently the other nodded and left, and Matt sank back on the pillows, feeling the unaccustomed softness of the bed under his body and surrendered himself to the weariness that crept over him once more.

How long did he have before the Chapmans came looking for him? Once they did pick up his trail from the camp, it would not be a difficult matter for them to trace this place and come looking for him there. He inwardly cursed the foolish carelessness that had almost cost him his life and had laid him up in bed with this shoulder wound at a time when he needed to be out and hunting down those polecats.

Helplessly he gritted his teeth, the muscles of his jaw lumping under the skin. In a little while his face began to ache and he forced himself to relax, but although it was possible for him to relax his body, there was no way to relax his mind. A host of thoughts kept popping into his brain, questions that demanded answers but for which he had no available answers which made sense.

With lawmen and outlaws both looking for him, what chance did he have of capturing the Chapman gang? The more he thought about it, the more hopeless it seemed. Even with Lynd's offer of help, he did not see that he would be able to go through with the tentative plans he had formulated in his mind. Tucson was a big, sprawling town, full of lawless men, and a stranger riding there was bound to attract some unwelcome attention.

It was with these thoughts in his mind that he finally fell into a deep and dreamless sleep.

5

Gunfight in Tucson

Matt Turner stood by the open window of the room, the heavy gunbelt buckled around his waist. His right hand and arm were still stiff and sore, although the bandages had been taken off that morning, but there was still the heaviness of pain in his muscles where they had been torn by the slashing bullet and had barely healed. In spite of this, he made his hand work. For almost an hour now he had stood there, alone in the room, methodically forcing life and movement back into arm and fingers.

Swiftly, evenly, his hand dropped to the butt of his gun, plucked and swept it upward while his finger tightened on the trigger and the hammer fell with a dull click on the empty chambers. With an effort, he forced himself to control the growing sense of coldness in his mind. Some day, very soon, he promised himself grimly, four men would stand in front of that gun and he would avenge the wrong they had done him.

Over and over again his hand dropped, lining up the barrel as the hammer clicked incessantly. Outside in the yard, he saw the girl walk over to the corral, thrust open the wooden gate, and step inside. One of the chestnut mares came over to her, nuzzling for the sugar she inevitably carried in her hand.

There was a slight sense of emptiness in him as he stood there with the faint coolness of the breeze sweeping round him. He stood for a long moment and watched her there, standing straight and slim and lovely in the flooding yellow sunlight. Maybe, he thought, the urges of a man who was used to riding the long trails alone and making his lonely camp under the stars at night, always at last moved and swung like a piece of lodestone in a compass towards the thought of a woman. Restlessness now bubbled up in his mind and a lot of the little things of the past few days came rushing up to the surface of his thoughts, little pictures and sounds which he thought had been forgotten. The harsh glare and searing hot touch of the desert sun on his back and shoulders during that long ride which had taken him back into Saddlerock — and trouble.

That faint rustle in the tall grass near a blazing camp fire when a man had tried to kill him and had himself died in the attempt. He forced the thoughts away with a conscious mental effort. These were the things he did not want to think about, not at that particular moment, anyway.

He knew that he could not afford to remain here at the Lynd ranch much longer. Already he had remained there for five days, since that morning when Rosaria Lynd had dragged him into the house, laid him out on the bed and taken that piece of lead out of his shoulder, cleaning the wound of the infection which had almost killed him.

Now he felt he had to be moving on into Tucson, hoping that it was not too late, and those outlaws had split up still further and moved on. If that had happened, it might be impossible for him ever to catch up with them, or even get a smell of their trail. For all he knew, their plans might have included a quick run for the border and over the frontier into Mexico.

Thrusting the Colt back into its holster, he pulled on his jacket and went out of the room, down the short flight of wooden stairs, through the kitchen and out into the courtyard. The full warmth of the sun hit him the moment he stepped outside and he began to feel better, more easy in his mind.

Slowly he made his way over to the fence of the corral and stood there, leaning his weight on his elbows, watching the girl idly. She felt his eyes on her, turned, then came forward with a smile, but the smile grew a little strained as her gaze fell and she noticed the guns at his waist.

'You're still determined to ride into Tucson today,' she said softly.

He nodded. 'I have to go,' he said simply. It was quietly said, but there was the promise of death in his words and in the way the tips of his fingers reached down, straight and taut, and touched the butts of his guns.

'Then nothing I can say will make you change your mind? Even though you know you would be safe here?'

'No.'

She gave him a quick, quizzical glance. 'You're a strange man, Matthew Turner,' she said gently. 'I'm not sure that I understand you — or what it is that drives you to this.'

'A man has to do what he thinks is right,' he said, shaping the words slowly and quietly. 'These men have made a criminal of me, a hunted man. How long do you think I could stay here, like a rat in a hole, hiding from the law, even running away from my own shadow, never knowing if those outlaws, or the law, might come riding by and spot me?'

'You're right, of course.' She seemed to change her mind abruptly.

If Matt felt any surprise at her sudden switch of ideas, he gave her no outward sign but continued to stare past her, out across the country which stretched clear to the eastern horizon. Although it looked good from where he stood, with plenty of lush grass and streams still a little swollen by the recent heavy rains, he knew that he had only to ride for perhaps ten miles before he hit the Badlands, the desert country where there was no water, and if a man lost himself there, he was finished, the buzzards picking his bones clean and white for the next lonely traveller to find.

But beyond the alkali desert lay Tucson and revenge. He pressed his lips tightly together, switched his glance to the girl and saw that she was looking directly at him appraisingly.

'I haven't thanked you properly for all of your hospitality,' he said softly.

'We've been glad to help.' She opened the corral gate and stepped through. There was something in her face, some expression at the back of her eyes, which he had never noticed there before. 'I wish you didn't have to go through with this. If they're waiting for you in Tucson . . . '

She let the hint of danger go unsaid, thereby giving it an added magnitude. Her words had sounded reluctant and resigned. 'Are you sure you know the men that you're looking for?'

He nodded. 'I know them now. Clayburn told me everything I needed to know. He's dead, but there are still the four others. Not until I've either killed them or taken them back to Saddlerock to stand trial for that stage robbery will I feel free again.'

She looked away, out over the

undulating hills that lay towards the east, then said quickly: 'But you will come back this way, if you succeed in what you have to do?'

'I'll come back,' he said tightly. For a moment he willed the gnawing hunger for action in his mind to be still. It was strange how easily a man could allow circumstances to blind him to reality, how he could let his emotions take a grip on him and run his life for him, how he could let the way he felt about something take hold of and distort the truth, make the right things look wrong, and hide the truth from him. He forced a faint sigh from his lips. If he were not careful a man could believe a great many foolish things about himself, think of himself as a man of peace, until something happened to show him that this image of himself had been only an exterior thing, a shell which covered the savage deep down inside. He could even believe that there was nothing left to his life but the need for revenge, the deep-seated desire to avenge a wrong which had been done him, when in reality there was something more . . .

★ ★ ★

The sun had already passed its zenith and was tracing a lowering path across the western heavens when he finally rode out of the Lynd ranch and headed east, over the lush grass of the stretching meadows, past the small stream that rippled down the slope between shallow banks, then through the small line of timber, out over the prairie which lay beyond and set his face towards the desert.

There was still a gnawing ache in his shoulder, but he forced himself to ignore it. The contours of the ground around him told him that he would reach the edge of the alkali within one hour, and there would still be sufficient heat in the sun to make the initial crossing uncomfortable. But the deep-seated urge for action had now risen in him in an irresistible wave and he did not try to fight it.

As he rode, a fine ashy dust began to puff up under the hooves of the sorrel, rose about them and settled on his sweating face, working its way in between the folds of his sweating skin, itching and irritating. He tried to wipe it away, but found it impossible. No sooner did he remove one layer than another formed on his flesh, and in the end he gave up the unequal struggle. Half an hour later he was well into the desert. Here there was no change in this land. The same flatness lay everywhere; the same sparse poverty of any vegetation, an occasional cactus, a few stunted mesquite or thorn bushes or green-brown patches of straggly grass. But there was little here that could not live with the minimum of moisture. Even though they might get torrential downpours of rain fifteen miles away near Saddlerock or Tucson, it never rained in this part of the country. It was as if the clouds were forced to shun this burning desert where the heat waves shimmered and danced all through the whole of the hot day, devising cruel and tantalising images of lakes and streams, mirages that were abruptly sucked up by the whirling dust devils which twisted and spun in their erratic courses over the desert. And during the night there was a deep and terrible coldness which soaked into a man's bones and made his flesh and muscles numb.

He sipped a few mouthfuls of water from his canteen, then thrust the water bottle back into his belt pouch. By nightfall he hoped to be more than halfway to Tucson. He knew that the burning ache in his shoulder was forcing him to travel at a far slower pace than he would normally have made; but that couldn't be helped.

The late afternoon sun struck him with heat from the side, and with the decline of the sun towards the western horizon at his back, a wind sprang up. But with the sun still above the horizon, it was not a cooling wind; rather it hurled scorching grains of sand against his face and eyes, half blinding him as he leaned forward in the saddle, head bowed low, eyes narrowed to mere slits, relying more and more on the horse to carry him forward in the right direction.

By nightfall his eyes were encrusted with sand, and it was difficult to see properly. A slim crescent of a moon floated in the sky and the air about him began to chill now that the sun had gone down, turning brittle with a cold that struck through his clothing and into his very bones. Coming so quickly after the scorching heat of the day only made it worse to bear. In the distance he heard the weirdly undulating howl of a coyote and the sound sent a little thrill through him as he became alert again.

The night was like tar except where the moon showed, and he had the feeling that he was all alone on the desert, that there was no other being within miles of him. Whenever he paused to listen, there was no sound other than the dry rustling sigh of the wind in the thorn bushes.

He camped in the darkness near an old buffalo run, rolling himself in his blankets to keep in a little of the warmth of his body, but in spite of the weariness and the discomfort in his body, it was a long while before he fell asleep. When he woke his body was chill and aching. It was still night and he forced himself to sit up and look about him. The moon had shifted a good deal and he knew that he had slept for several hours, that soon it would be dawn.

Drinking down a little of his remaining water, he saddled up, swung up weakly into the saddle and moved off into the still darkness. Presently the horizon ahead of him was lighting up. A greyish yellow light was streaking the skyline, spreading slowly across his line of vision like a faint seeping of blood. He looked out across the flat land and soon made out the faint dark blotch on the landscape that was the town of

Tucson. It still lay the best part of ten miles distant, but he estimated that with luck he would make it there by high noon. He gave the sorrel its head, content to sit upright in the saddle, eyes alert.

Then, to his right, and on the horizon, he saw the silhouettes of distant riders. He pulled sharply on the reins, wheeling his mount in the opposite direction, to keep as much distance between them and himself as possible. At the moment he did not particularly wish to have company. He kept them in sight until they had moved away into the distance, then moved his attention to the ground ahead of him. By now the desert sun had lifted clear of the horizon, beating down mercilessly on him. Time seemed to become a tenuous and apparently endless thing, minutes stretching themselves out into long individual eternities. He tried to estimate the passage of time by the diminishing distance between himself and the dark shadow of the town.

High noon and he was riding slowly down the main street of Tucson. Here he knew his way around, but on the outskirts of the town, nailed to a tree beside the trail, he had spotted a wanted poster with his picture on it and offering a reward of a thousand dollars for his capture, dead or alive. The discovery of that grim picture had made him realise just how vulnerable he was now that he had ridden into town. His only hope was to find those men as quickly as possible and then get out equally quickly unless one of them could be made to talk to the sheriff.

Tucson was still something of a lawless town. The big cattle bosses brought their herds through the town to the cattle pens around the railhead, and whenever this happened their men moved in on the town in a last wild fling before heading out on to the trail again. He was aware of the faces which turned and eyed him curiously as he rode along the dusty street with the full heat of the sun lying like the pressure of some mighty hand over everything. He tried to ignore them, telling himself that not everyone could have seen that poster, and those who had would scarcely believe he would be so foolish as to come riding brazenly into town in this way. A little thought brought a quirk to his lips as he remembered that he had been accused of such a thing back in Saddlerock just before the sheriff had taken him away and locked him up in the jail.

With the heat of the day full on the town, he guessed that if any of the Chapman gang were in Tucson, then the logical place to start looking for them would be in one of the saloons dotted along the length of the main street. There was a crowd of men inside the first he came to, but although he examined every face he saw there, none of them belonged to the men he was seeking.

At one of the small stores he put some discreet questions to the white-haired man at the back of the plain wooden counter, but the other shook his head slowly, intimated that he had never seen men answering to the descriptions he gave. He asked at one or two other places before moving on to the next saloon, but always the answer was the same, although he had the feeling that one of the men he asked was hiding something, knew more than he told. There had been a crafty glint in the other's eye as Matt spoke to him, and as he came out of the shop into the street and swung himself up into the saddle, he wondered if he had not been too open about this and whether there might not be someone here who would move along and warn the Chapman brothers if they did happen to be somewhere in the town. He shrugged his shoulders a little as he moved out into the street once more. If that was the case, then the damage was done.

★　★　★

Ed Chapman rested his heavily built frame on the edge of the bar, resting his weight on his elbows. Beside him, Clem Chapman, more slightly built, tilted the whisky bottle and spilled the brown liquid into his glass, then lifted the brimming rim to his lips and drank, wiping the back of his hand across his mouth.

He paused for a moment, then said harshly: 'What do you make of it, Ed? You figure Turner did get sprung outa jail and he has killed Clayburn?'

'Mebbe.' The other spoke in a harsh grunt of sound, hands tightly clenched on the bar in front of him. 'If he has, then he'll be headed this way, and as soon as he gets into Tucson, I'll kill him.'

He poured himself another glass and tossed it down in one quick gulp. Behind them, the batwing doors were suddenly thrust open and a man in a white apron came into the saloon, cast about him rapidly with an almost frightened look on his face, spotted the two brothers at the bar and hurried over to them, thrusting his way between the tables and the men gathered around them. Panting a little, he came up to the bar and stood beside Ed Chapman.

'Mister Chapman,' he said breathlessly. 'I — '

Chapman whirled on him savagely. 'What do you want, Carew?' he snapped thinly. 'Can't you see that I'm drinking here with my brother?'

The other winced almost as if the outlaw had struck him. Then he moistened his lips, stood his ground with an effort and went on quickly, the words spilling out, one after the other, in a torrent, as if he thought he might not have the chance to finish what he had to say.

'I'm sorry, Mister Chapman, but this is important. There's an hombre just come riding into town asking for the whereabouts of four men, and two of 'em sounded remarkably like you. I figured you ought to know about it.'

'What does he look like?' muttered

Chapman tightly. He threw a quick, enigmatic glance at his brother.

Swiftly, the shopkeeper described Turner. When he had finished, Chapman gave a quick nod. 'So he's finally got here,' he muttered through his teeth. 'It looks like that story we heard about him was true after all.' He took a coin from his pocket and tossed it ringingly on to the bar, calling loudly to the barkeep:

'A drink for my friend here, bartender. Anything he wants.' He moved away from the bar, taking his brother by the arm and leading him to one of the tables, where he sank down into a chair. Throwing a quick look in the direction of the door, he said hoarsely: 'He's played right into our hands now, Clem. As soon as he walks through that door, we'll nail him.' A note of grim amusement entered his coarse voice as he added: 'Might be that we'll collect that thousand dollars reward after all.'

★ ★ ★

170

Outside the saloon, Matt dismounted slowly, stood for a moment beside the sorrel where he could see in both directions along the dusty, sun-hazed street without being easily seen himself. He studied the faces of the men on the boardwalk and the few who rode past while he stood there, but he recognised none of them. One man riding past had a deputy's star pinned on his shirt, glinting brilliantly in the harsh sunglare, and he waited until the other had reined his mount in front of the sheriff's office some two hundred yards further down the street and gone inside the building before he moved out into the open and stood eyeing the saloon for a moment. Something puzzled him now. Out of the corner of his eye he had noticed one of the shopkeepers he had spoken with slip out of the side entrance of the shop as soon as the other had figured that his back was turned and hurry along the boardwalk, still wearing his white apron, making it a simple matter to pick out his hurrying figure against the rest of the townsfolk. The man had vanished inside this saloon, throwing a wary glance along the street before he had pushed open the doors and vanished from sight.

Matt could feel the little knot of tension beginning to harden in the pit of his stomach. There was danger here. He could feel it crackling in the air. If the Chapman gang were inside the saloon, they would have been warned by now of his presence in the town, would know that he had come looking for them and that, with Clayburn dead, he was something to be reckoned with. Accordingly, the chances were that they were on the other side of those batwing doors at that very moment with their guns lined up, ready to drill him with lead the minute he pushed the doors open and stepped inside.

For a long moment he stood there, studying the place. There was a balcony which ran around the top storey, circling the four sides of the building. If he could get up there without being seen from the street, he stood a good chance of moving into the top floor and taking the outlaws by surprise.

Carefully, he stepped across the boardwalk and moved around to the side of the saloon. The alley was narrow, and at the back there were piles of evil-smelling garbage. Swarms of flies hovered over them and he wrinkled his nostrils as the stench came floating up to him. With an effort he ignored it, went back and brought the sorrel around. Pushing the flanks of the horse well in under the overhanging balcony, he paused for a moment, then swung himself up into the saddle. From there he found he could reach one of the wooden supporting posts and used it for a balance to keep himself upright as he stood in the saddle. There was a second when the horse shied away from under him, but he made soft clucking noises and it steadied almost instantly. Bringing up first one foot and then the other, he was able to stand upright in the saddle, holding on to the supporting post with both hands. Gritting his teeth as he took the strain on his injured shoulder, he pulled himself up, hanging on grimly as his fingers threatened to loose their hold on the smooth wood. Sweat popped out on his forehead and began to drip down into his eyes, stinging and half blinding him, but he knew that now he had committed himself to this manoeuvre, he had to go through with it, whatever happened. From the direction of the street he could hear the sudden thunder of hooves as a group of riders went tearing along the main street. At the far end of town he heard them loosing off their guns and the sharp barks of gunshots, followed by the echoes that chased themselves among the buildings deadened any noise he made as, with a tremendous heave of his shoulder muscles, he pulled himself over the lip of the balcony and fell, sprawling, on to the woodwork below.

Slowly, painfully, he hauled himself to his feet, stood for a long moment not daring to draw breath, listening for any movement inside the room less than three feet from where he stood, the window half open. Setting his teeth as pain jarred along his right arm, he edged forward, paused outside the window, then drew aside the filmy lace curtains and climbed into the room.

He was still breathing hard, the air rasping in his lungs and along his burning throat. But he was inside the saloon by an entrance which those men downstairs would not have considered, and the room he found himself in was empty.

Quickly he moved over to the door, turned the handle very slowly and quietly, opened it just a crack and peered out into the passage that lay beyond. It was empty and a deep silence seemed to lie over everything. It was too quiet for Matt's liking, but he could not know what was happening downstairs in the saloon itself. Hefting his gun into his right hand, he stepped out and walked swiftly along the passage, his booted heels making no sound in the thick carpet on the floor.

At the end of the passage he found himself, as he had guessed, at the top of the stairs. Cautiously he peered down over the low balcony. The place was crowded with men. Most of the tables were full, with some playing dice, others poker, some merely drinking, trying to slake their thirst in the heat of the day.

Slowly, carefully, he ran his gaze along the men standing at the bar, but recognised none of them. Then he shifted his glance to the men seated at the tables scattered throughout the room and, a moment later, felt a sudden leap of feeling in his body as he spotted Ed and Clem Chapman seated at one of the tables facing the doors. They had their backs to him, their hands above the table and each man held a sixgun in his fist, fingers on the trigger. He smiled grimly to himself as he stood there, staring down. His guess had been correct and it had obviously saved his life. The minute he stepped through those doors down there he would have been a dead man without a chance to go for his guns. But if that was the way these polecats wanted to play, then by God that was the way they would get it. He wanted to shoot them both in the back while he was sure, knowing in himself that neither man deserved any better, but that kind of killing was not in him.

Reaching the top of the stairs, he paused there for a moment, then stiffened as one of the men at the bar happened to glance up and catch sight of him. The man opened his mouth but before he could let out his yell of warning, Matt's voice rang out loud and clear above the general sound in the saloon:

'You two killers waiting for me?'

The effect was instantaneous. Both Chapmans whirled and turned to face him, the guns in their hands, jerking in his general direction, although it was clear they did not see him at first. Then the two men spotted him and threw themselves sideways from the table, the chairs going over as their weight fell clumsily against them. In the same instant the guns in Matt's hands spoke and the slugs ploughed into the wooden top of the table at which the men had been seated a moment earlier. He went down on one knee as gunfire lanced up at him. Two men near the bar were also firing at him and he heard the bullets hum close to his head and imbed themselves in the woodwork at his back.

Sighting swiftly, not noticing the pain in his shoulder now, he loosed off a volley of shots, squeezing the triggers continually, saw Clem Chapman, still sprawled on the floor halfway under the table, suddenly jerk and stiffen as one of the slugs took him in the chest. He dropped his gun from nerveless fingers and lay still.

Cursing loudly and savagely, Ed

Chapman threw himself out of Matt's line of fire, dropping down at the back of the table, overturning it and thrusting it up as barricade for himself.

Matt tightened his lips. Down below most of the saloon had miraculously cleared as the majority of the customers moved for the doors and tumbled out into the street or dropped out of sight behind the long bar.

A man crouched down near the doorway fired up at him, pitched forward as a bullet caught him in the neck. Even as he died on his feet, his finger pressed down on the trigger of his sixgun with the last ounce of strength left in him and the bullet smashed into the long glass mirror at the back of the bar, shattering it into a hundred shining pieces which crowded down on the men lying flat on their faces on the floor.

Matt narrowed his gaze, trying to pick out the whereabouts of Ed Chapman. He could not see him behind the overturned table where he had been a few moments earlier. Then he caught a fragmentary glimpse of the outlaw heading around the far end of the bar. Matt loosed off a couple of shots after the fleeing outlaw, saw them miss by inches as the other scurried like an animal over the floor on his hands and knees.

Then the hammers of his guns clicked onimously on empty chambers. Cursing savagely, he drew away from the edge of the balcony, pushed more slugs into the chambers of the sixers from the pouches in his belt. Bullets fled up from the room below, chirruping along the top of the balcony, and he heard harsh yells and orders from the saloon. A few moments later a small knot of men began to move in the direction of the bottom of the stairs, no doubt encouraged by the momentary lack of fire from up there. He drew in a deep breath, knew that he would not stand much of a chance against this hornet's nest that he had aroused. There was no doubt that Clem

Chapman was dead. He could just make out the younger outlaw's body lying face downward on the floor by the overturned table. He had not moved an inch since Matt's bullet had taken him in the chest.

But Ed Chapman, the more dangerous of the two outlaws, had gone. Somehow he had managed to slip out unnoticed through the door situated at the far end of the bar. Gritting his teeth together until the muscles of his jaw lumped under the flesh, he edged back from the balcony, sent a handful of shots whistling into the body of men getting ready to rush him, then ran swiftly along the corridor, back into the empty room he had entered a little while before, throwing all caution to the winds now. Outside, the narrow alley seemed empty and deserted and the sorrel was still standing in its original position.

Forcing away the feeling of sickness that rose in his body whenever he jarred the muscles of his injured shoulder, he clambered over the balcony, stood poised for a moment, hanging on to the upright with both hands, then took a deep breath and released his hold. He landed awkwardly on the back of the horse, felt it move from under him, almost sending him sprawling in the dust. Jerking air into his heaving lungs, he clung on to the saddle, swung himself up into it with a heave that tore at his shoulder and arm and brought the sweat out on his face and neck.

There was confused shouting from the front of the saloon and he guessed that some of the men would still be spilling out with news of the shooting inside. Not long now before the sheriff and a handful of deputies arrived on the scene, he decided. Time to get out while he still had the chance.

He urged the mount away from the saloon, moving around to the rear of the building, and it was as he broke out into the narrow street at the back that he spotted the dark figure running furtively along the side of the street towards a couple of horses which had been tethered a few yards away in the distance.

The man turned as he heard the clatter of hooves at his back, saw Matt and recognised him instantly. He jerked up the gun from his belt and squeezed off a couple of quick shots as he lengthened his stride, running now for the horses.

Matt tried to pluck his own gun from its holster, but the sorrel reared savagely as one of the bullets sliced across its chest. It was all that he could do to hold on and prevent himself from being thrown from the saddle. Dimly, he heard the clatter of hooves as the other man rode swiftly away, kicking up dust as he did so. Before he could recover control of the sorrel, the other had vanished around the corner of the buildings some distance ahead, and Matt knew instinctively that he would be lost among the crowd in the main street and he would never find him. For the moment he would have to be content with killing one of the Chapman brothers.

He wheeled his mount, rode swiftly along the narrow road out towards the edge of town, listening for any sound of pursuit. There was some yelling still going on around the saloon, but it faded as he put more distance between it and himself. He would be lucky if he didn't have a sheriff's posse on his heels before dark, and besides Ed Chapman, who would be nursing a passionate desire for revenge for the slaying of his brother, there were the other two members of the gang to be taken into account. Where were they at this moment? It was possible they were not even in Tucson. For all he knew, they could have split up some days before and the other two had ridden out, leaving only Ed and Clem in town. But he did not doubt that before long Ed Chapman would find those other two and the three of them would come hunting him.

As he reached the edge of town he

searched the winding trail ahead of him for any sign of Ed Chapman. But the other was nowhere in sight. Having realized that Matt was a far tougher proposition than he had at first thought, the other had quickly disappeared, evidently deciding that there would be another time and another place for revenge.

Gigging the sorrel, he rode quickly along the trail leading to the west. Glancing down, he was surprised to find that his hands were trembling a little as they gripped the reins with a more than usual tightness. The skin felt tight and pinched on his face as if it had shrunk and drawn itself down closer on to the bones of his cheeks. He waited until he rounded a sharp bend in the trail, then let his breath out long and low, easing the pain in his chest. Tension still held his body in a hard grip, but it began to ease slowly and his mind, which he had automatically locked against thought, broke again into motion and he found a strange sense of relief flooding through him.

He shifted his weight more evenly in the saddle, spat out the dust in his mouth, felt a little stirring of the tension as he realised that there was dust hanging in the air, indicating that a rider had passed this way recently and had been travelling fast.

Ed Chapman?

He let the thought trickle idly through his mind. It was possible, he reflected. Unless the other had mingled with the crowd in the main street and decided it would be safer for him to remain behind in town, where he would be just one of the crowd, rather than ride hell for leather out here into the open where he could be spotted for several miles, where he would lift a dust wake that would label his passing as clearly as if he had left a trail.

Twenty minutes later he mounted a low rise, halted the sorrel and stared over the stretching country which lay spread in front of him in the afternoon sunlight.

Far in the distance, very close to

the skyline, he spotted the diminishing dust cloud, now no bigger than a man's hand. Too far for him to hope to overtake the other. If it was Chapman, he seemed to be in a big hurry. There had been plenty of places along that part of the trail where the other could have laid an ambush for him. On the other hand, if Chapman were heading for his other two companions, determined to outnumber him the next time they met, and not to make the same mistake, then it seemed only logical that he would ride fast and keep on riding through the day and night until he linked up with them. He would not even stop to make camp for fear that the same thing happened to him as had happened to Clayburn and those other two killers.

Once he realised this, Matt kept the sorrel at a steady pace. The sun was still high but the shadowed patches of ground were lengthened and there was plenty of shade among the tall, towering buttes.

By the time he edged his way over the rim of the desert, skirting it this time further to the north, there was no sign of the other rider. He had ridden fast over the horizon, would possibly be halfway to Saddlerock now, if he were, indeed, heading in that direction.

Along the southern edge of the alkali flats he linked up with the broad stage trail and rode more quickly along it. He would make good time on this trail, but there could be trouble. It would be frequented much more than that straight ride across the desert, and he would have to keep his eyes peeled.

He made a long ride before nightfall, then made lonely camp half a mile from the trail in the lee of a small hill. He did not know much of this country, but that made little difference to him. He had ridden trails like this far more years than he cared to remember, and found himself at home wherever night came upon him. He built a small fire and sat just on the edge of the red glow.

6

First Warning

When he stepped into the saddle the next morning his body a little refreshed by the rest, he rode parallel to the stage trail. At intervals during the later part of the night, he had been wakened by the sound of riders coming and going along the trail, and he guessed that, with a price on his head, it would not be wise for him to stick too close to the stage road. Looking to his right, he made out the rolling leagues of the desert, stretching away as far as the eye could see, and he was glad he had not chosen to ride that trail.

Even here, on the rim of the Badlands, the ground was rough with patches of scrub, and darting sand lizards giving the only flash of colour to be seen in that drab world. They were of almost every conceivable colour, these swiftly streaking creatures, green, gold and purple. Occasionally he would notice one of them atop a mount of smooth rock, eyeing him unwinkingly as he approached, not moving an inch even as he drew level with it, only a few feet away. Then, abruptly, without any warning, it would twitch its tail and dart off into the shadows, a blur of colour that was swiftly gone.

He rode with a rider's looseness in his limbs, eyes half-hidden behind lowered lids to shield out some of the sun's glare. As yet he had made no definite plans in his head as to what he would do once he reached Saddlerock, which was his next destination. If he found Ed Chapman or any of the other members of the gang there, it might be wisest to go straight to Sheriff Hogan and warn him of the position. Whether he could still trust the other to feel the same way about him, especially if he had heard about the shooting out in the desert, he did not know. Maybe after he had let him go, the sheriff had had second thoughts on the matter and was now regretting the incident.

Shortly before noon he came on a small ranch headquarters, standing in the lee of a small hill where a deep valley had been cut into the rolling plain in long ages past. There was an abundance of green grass here and he noticed a small herd of cattle on the lower slopes of the hill.

House and barn came into view as he turned the narrow trail around the base of the hill, and when he got nearer he saw the two men standing on the porch. The nearer man was heavy and tall, broad-shouldered, face tanned brown by long exposure to sun. The other man, shorter but wiry, face like leather, had the same kind of features, stamped with tar from the same brush, the same high-bridged nose and piercing blue eyes.

Both fastened coolly inhospitable glances on him and for a moment, as he reined his mount in front of the porch, he thought he saw a look of crafty appraisal come into the smaller man's eyes. Meanwhile, he sat in the saddle and waited patiently for the offer to dismount. It was a long time in coming. The big man seemed to speculate on him for longer than usual, then he gave a quick, curt nod.

'Better get down from your horse for a spell, man, get out of the sun,' he said.

Matt swung easily from the saddle, stretched, flexing the muscles of his legs, cramped a little by so much riding. There was the bitter taste of dust in his mouth and throat, and although he rolled himself a smoke, he did not light it, but stood with it between his fingers, letting his gaze drift from one man to the other.

The big man said finally: 'You just riding through, mister, or you got business in these parts?' He spoke with a certain arrogance, the words sharp and distinct, not slow and slurred like those of a real Westerner.

Matt said, glancing at the herd on the

lee side of the hill: 'This your outfit?'

The other nodded. 'We're partners in this, both have a half share, if that's what you're gettin' at.'

'Always like to know who I'm talking to,' said Matt softly. He lit the cigarette now and drew smoke deep into his lungs, grimacing a little as it burned his lips where they were cracked and parched.

The shorter man twisted his lips into a wintry smile, meeting Matt's steady look with one of puzzled apprehension. 'You look like just another bum to me, stranger, a saddle-tramp probably with the law close behind you. Just a crook trying to make it into the hills around Saddlerock before a sheriff's posse puts a bullet into you.'

The look of grim amusement on his lips faded quickly, to be replaced by an almost expectant expression. 'Ain't I seen you some place before?'

Matt dragged the smoke of the cigarette deep into his lungs, then blew it out. 'I doubt it. I've never been in these parts before.'

The man gave him a prolonged study. The remark seemed to be of some interest to him and he rubbed his fingers over his chin as if something about Matt had quickened his attention. His glance was a pushing one, probing Matt's face as if seeking something familiar. Then he shook his head, jerked a thumb towards the back of the building.

'There's water around the back. Drink your fill. Better let your mount have some, too. You look as if you've ridden a long way.'

'Pretty far,' agreed Matt tersely. He caught the reins and led the sorrel around to the rear of the ranch. He found the wide trough at the side of the house, let the horse drink a little, then bent and allowed the thin stream from the pipe to run into his mouth, swallowing greedily, then forced himself to stop. It was not as much as he wanted, nor as much for the horse either. But they had the worst of the day still in front of them and it was far better to ride dry than to sweat out water all the day, better for both man and beast.

He went back to the porch. The two men were still there. Quite evidently they had been talking about him for they stopped the minute he appeared.

'You want a job?' asked the big man abruptly.

'Riding with you, or fighting?'

The other shrugged negligently.

'More of one and less of the other.'

'You seen a man riding through this way earlier?'

The other narrowed his eyes. 'What did he look like?'

'Big, like you. Black-bearded, rough-looking. Riding fast to Saddlerock.'

'Nope. Ain't seen anybody answerin' to that description. You lookin' for him?'

'Could be. Thanks for the drink.'

'You look like you could do with a rest. Care to shack up here for a few days?'

'Got to be moving along,' said Matt, very dry.

'Least you could rest up for the rest of the day,' pointed out the other. 'Wait until the heat head is past. Your horse looks as if it could do with a rest up for a few hours. Your man ain't going to run much in the next few hours.'

Matt thought that over, mulling it over in his mind. It would not do too much harm to accept that offer, he thought to himself, and there was something in what the other said. Besides, if his mount was rested until the worst of the day was past, he would make much better time during the night. After high noon the heat head would reach the peak of its piled up intensity and he did not really relish the idea of riding through it.

'I'd be glad to accept the offer for the rest of the day,' he said, crushing out his smoke. 'But whatever happens, I'll have to be riding on tonight.'

'Sure, sure,' nodded the other. 'There's a bunk in the spare room at the back and we'll stable your mount until nightfall.'

★　★　★

Matt was wakened some time during the early part of the afternoon by a sound outside the window of his room. He lay for a moment, dragging himself up from the depths of exhausted sleep, then swung his legs to the floor and stood up, going over to the window, moving noiselessly. Keeping his body pressed against the wall so as not to be seen by anyone outside, he glanced through the window. The sun was still very close to the zenith and there were few shadows in the yard at the back of the house. For a moment he could see nothing and there was no repetition of the sound that had wakened him, reaching down through his mind to the part which never slept.

Then he heard the faint sound at the corner of the house and pushed his head forward a little further. The murmur of conversation reached him a moment later as the two men came into view. One was leading his horse by the reins, taking care to make as little sound as possible. He drew back quickly as they halted and both lifted their heads to stare up at the window of his room. For a long moment he stood there, scarcely daring to breathe, not quite knowing what the danger was from these two men, although the feeling was there in his mind that some kind of danger threatened him.

Carefully he let the air go from his lungs, saw that they had moved off a little and some of their words floated up to him in the stillness:

'I tell you I did recognise him,' murmured the smaller man. 'I'm sure of it. They brought the posters a coupla days ago and nailed 'em to the tree along the trail half a mile back. It's Matt Turner all right, wanted for that stage hold-up in Saddlerock.'

'But he said he was riding into

Saddlerock after some hombre,' protested the other. 'If he was a wanted man, it ain't likely he'd do that. Only a fool would ride into trouble, deliberately stickin' his neck out.'

'Mebbe he's not such a big fool as we think,' went on the other. 'You ride on into Saddlerock, warn Sheriff Hogan that he's here. I'll try to stall him as long as I can, but ride hell for leather and don't stop on the way back. If he once begins to suspect, there may be trouble.'

'I won't stop,' nodded the other. He moved his mount further away from the house, then stepped up into the saddle, bent a little and said something to the other, but they were too far away for Matt to pick out anything of their conversation.

A few moments later the big man rode off and there was only a diminishing cloud of dust to mark his trail. Matt went back into the room and seated himself on the edge of the bunk. He had half suspected that these two hombres had had some kind of motive for wanting him to rest up there. It had not been in keeping with the welcome he had first received on riding into the ranch. The little man must have recognised him easily, but kept the fact to himself until he was sure he could not be overheard.

There was no doubt that he would have to ride out — and fast. Once the big man hit town, he would lose no time in appraising the sheriff of what had happened and this time Hogan would be forced to ride out with the posse and bring him in.

Going over to the chest of drawers, he picked up the heavy leather gunbelt and fastened it tightly around his middle. He still felt a little unsure about what to do with the man downstairs. He didn't want to kill him unless he had to. He was becoming sick of killing men, yet the deeper he seemed to get into this, the more men he had to kill. But he had to get away before the man's partner arrived back with the law.

Going to the door, he stood for a long moment, listening for any sound of movement outside, but he could hear nothing. Carefully he turned the knob and opened the door just a little. A moment later he heard the other in the kitchen moving the pots around.

Smiling grimly to himself, he walked down the narrow stairs, through into the kitchen. The other had his back to him as he went inside, did not seem to have heard him; then seemed to sense his presence for he whirled sharply, a little guiltily.

'Sorry if I startled you,' said Matt easily. He gave the other a quick glance. 'I heard somebody ride off and it must've woken me.' He walked to the door, deliberately turning his back on the other, but still watchful and alert, still expecting trouble. But the man made no move toward the guns at his belt.

Pausing in the doorway, Matt threw a quick look at the sky. Then he turned and said: 'Guess I ought to be moving

on now. I've intruded on your hospitality too long. The sorrel ought to be
rested pretty well now and — '

'But you'll stay for a bite to eat,'
broke in the other, a trifle too quickly.

Matt shook his head. 'Got a lot of
ground to cover. Best I get started
now. Should reach Saddlerock before
sundown.'

'But the heat head is at its worst right
now.' The other looked at him in
surprise, but there was something else
at the back of his eyes, and he spoke his
words just a little too swiftly, anxious to
put forward some argument.

'Where's your partner gone?' Matt
spoke evenly. 'I guess it was him I heard
ride out a little while ago.'

'Sure, it was Jake. He thought he'd
better take a look at the herd. We ain't
got no help right now and we take it in
turn to check on the cattle. Been some
rustlin' in these parts over the past few
weeks. Got to protect 'em if we can.'

Matt gave no outward sign that he
knew the other was lying, but pressed

his lips together, gave a quick nod. 'You must be kept pretty busy.' From where he stood it was just possible for him to make out the herd on the side of the hill less than a mile away. There was no sign of any rider there and the other came over and stood beside him looking over his shoulder.

'Reckon I'll pick my mount out of the corral,' he said, turning. He forced himself to walk slowly over the hard dust of the courtyard to the corral, paused by the gate, then whistled shrilly. The sorrel, on the far side of the corral, lifted its head, saw him, and came galloping over. He led it into the courtyard and threw the saddle over it, tightening the cinch under the horse's belly. As he bent, he threw a swiftly apprehensive glance in the direction of the ranch, wondering when the other would make his play and how he would try to keep him there. There was, of course, the chance that the man might decide to do nothing about it, just to let him ride out, and warn the posse when they got there, believing that there was no sense in him risking his life for the sake of bringing in a wanted killer. On the other hand, he might try to take him himself.

He straightened up, saw that the man had moved out of the house, stood straddle-legged a few yards away in the glaring sunlight, his hands held out from his body, his fingers stiff like the spokes of a wheel. Matt looked at him, locking his gaze with the other's. The man's brows were drawn down into a straight line over his blue eyes and he licked his lips a little as he stood there. Watching him, Matt saw the beading of sweat that had formed on his forehead, a little running down his cheeks and dripping from his chin.

'You got somethin' on your mind?' Matt asked.

'What makes you think that?' demanded the other. He spoke a trifle more truculently than he had evidently intended.

'You seem to be getting ready to call me,' Matt grinned thinly. He moved away from his mount, out into the open, where he had freedom of movement. 'I reckoned that you might have recognised me from one of those posters they've spread out over the territory. That's why you sent your partner hightailing it into Saddlerock to warn the sheriff. It may surprise you to know that it was Sheriff Hogan who let me out of jail in Saddlerock when that mob there wanted to lynch me. His brother was one of those deputies shot by the bandits and it ain't likely he'd have let me go if he figured I was one of 'em.'

'I only got your word for any of that,' said the other slowly. 'Reckon you'd say anything like that when you was in a tight spot.'

'You figure I'm in a tight spot?' Matt queried. The other was still stalling for time. There was a brightness in his eyes, but the sun was burning down directly into his face, and Matt knew that he had the edge on the rancher if he tried to do anything.

'Those wanted posters ask for you dead or alive,' persisted the other. 'And they're offerin' a thousand dollars. Reckon they must be pretty sure of themselves.'

'Then I reckon that if you figure you can earn yourself that thousand dollar reward, you'd better make your play.' There was no amusement in Matt's tone now. He had noticed the slight change that had come to the other's face. He stared at him steadily, holding the rancher's glance, murmuring in a soft little voice: 'I don't want to have to kill you, mister, but I will if I have to, make no mistake about that.'

He saw the man hesitate. His tongue came out, running around his lips once more, and this time his eyes did not seem to be locking so well with Matt's. It was plain that the other considered himself to be a tough hombre, that he was ready and willing to answer any challenge thrown at him. But now that the situation was no longer just one in his mind, one that he dreamed about; now that it was a reality, he was no longer so sure of himself. He had a belief in himself, but it was a belief that had been based on his imagination.

Matt stood absolutely still and watched the battle that was going on inside the man; a battle for courage and self-respect. The other knew that within the next minute or so he would have to answer that challenge, would have to discover for himself, whether he had any spark of manhood left in him, or whether his pride and courage had turned yeasty inside him. Matt saw the strange putty lines about the man's face, felt his own lips curl disdainfully as he thrust the Colts deeper into their holsters, turning away a little.

'You ain't even got the guts to shoot me in the back,' he said with purpose. He stepped up into the saddle. 'But thanks for that warning about Saddle-rock. I reckon I know where to ride now.'

He gave a short, sharp laugh, touched spurs to his horse's flanks and galloped quickly out of the courtyard, taking the trail back east, in the direction of Tucson. Glancing back over his shoulder as he cleared the edge of the courtyard, he saw the small figure of the rancher still standing there in the harsh, flooding sunlight, eyeing him from beneath the brim of his hat. There was something oddly pathetic about that man, he reflected idly, as he turned in the saddle. It might have been the same way when Sheriff Hogan had let him out of the jail and told him to ride into the night. He could have kept on riding into the darkness, taken a trail which would have carried him well clear of the hills, and kept on riding until he was miles away, in a different state altogether, where he might have tried to settle down under a new identity.

But he hadn't. Instead, he had turned and fought. So it could have been with that rancher back there. One yell might have saved him. A swift move towards the guns in his belt, even if he had not succeeded in killing Matt, he would have preserved his dignity and manhood, for Matt doubted if he could have shot him down. A slug in the shoulder or the arm would have stopped him. That man had been no gunman, no killer.

He forgot the man almost immediately, concentrated on what lay ahead for him. Now that he came to review the situation, it had certain advantages. With the posse heading out from Saddlerock, and with that rancher undoubtedly telling them that he had known of their plan and had ridden out in the direction of Tucson, they would doubtless think he had headed in that direction, and Saddlerock could be the safest place for him to hide, the last place they would ever think of looking for him.

Half a mile from the ranch, when he was well out of sight of the place, he left the trail, climbed into the towering rocks and then cut back along the fringe of the desert, heading in a wide circle to the west. He took care to ride clear of the trail, and two hours later, with the sun beginning to trace a burning arc down the western sky, he spotted the dust cloud that hazed the horizon in the direction of the trail. He reined his mount behind a narrow fringe of timber, sat tall in the saddle and watched them come on, a bunch of riders spurring their mounts to the limit; men in a hurry, determined to catch the man they believed had been among the stage robbers, the man who had busted out of jail.

They rode by, keeping to the trail, not pausing for a single instant. He sat there until they had passed out of sight, then gigged his mount and rode on, heading for Saddlerock. It would be at least four hours before the posse returned to town, and by that time it would be sundown.

He came into town by a narrow, winding trail, deliberately avoiding the main street. The sun had vanished behind the western hills in a flash of red and scarlet, and already it was getting dark as the short twilight ended. There were lights in the windows of several of the houses and the saloons. And in the hotel he could make out the room which he had occupied when he had first ridden into town, when there had been no suspicions against him. His saddle roll and bags would still be there, waiting for him to claim them, unless they had been taken over and his room let to someone else.

He rode slowly between the squat-roofed houses along the narrow street, where the lights shone dimly through windows which seemed to be eternally coated with the white dust that blew off the prairie. Halfway along the street, before it linked with the main street at the intersection, he found a small livery stable and drew into it, keeping his face in darkness as a man drifted out from the rear, took his horse from him as he dismounted. The other tried to peer closely at him, then drew back a little.

'Take care of the sorrel,' Matt said to the livery man. 'We've ridden a long way and he may need a rub down before you feed him.'

'Sure thing,' the other nodded, chewing thoughtfully on a wad of tobacco. He led the horse away and Matt hung his gear on one of the pegs on the wall near the entrance, then moved out into the street, the soft, sweet smell of the hay still in his nostrils, a pleasant change from the harsh alkali dust that had been with him most of his travels. The night wind was blowing down off the hills, cooling the heat of the day from his body, but it could not ease the tightness in his limbs as he thought of the price that had been placed on his head, knew that there would be many people in Saddlerock, not only the remaining three members of the Chapman gang, who would want to see him dead, might shoot him down on sight if they recognised him.

Pausing near the long drinking trough, he let the cool water from the feed pipe slide down his parched throat and fill his body until it could hold no more. It brought a little sweat out on his body, chilling instantly in the cool air.

There were few people in the street. With the sheriff and a posse out looking for him at that ranch, things seemed slack. He would still have to tread very warily around town. The few men on the boardwalk, passing him, gave him a quick, curious glance, then moved on. It was a noticeable thing, the way they eyed him, even though they could make out little of his features in the shadows of the street.

Rounding the corner, he caught the sharp odour of food from a small hotel set a little way back from the square. This was obviously supper hour and a slack time in the street of the town. He rolled himself a cigarette, although he had no need of one, and stood for a long moment in the shadows of the buildings, watching the front of the small hotel. A handful of men moved idly in and out as he watched, moving to and from supper and, acting on impulse, he tossed the unlit cigarette on to the boardwalk, roughed it with his heel, then crossed the street and went inside the hotel, going directly into the dining room. The trail dust was still on him, marking him out as a man who had just ridden into town. It caked his lean jaw and the flesh of his cheeks, and provided him with a form of mask against closely prying eyes.

It was soon apparent that he need not have worried himself on that particular score. He ordered his meal, paid for it, seated with his face towards the door of the dining room. He ate slowly, relishing the taste of good food, washing it down with the hot, strong coffee. Finally he sat back in his chair, deliberately relaxed, muscles loose, surrendering slightly to the laziness and luxury that came at the end of a long ride.

He smoked a cigarette slowly, still keeping his gaze fastened on the door. No danger yet. Pushing back his chair, he got to his feet, hitched the heavy gunbelt a little higher around his middle with his thumbs, then went out into the street. Tension grew in him as he moved slow-footed through the dust towards the square. It was just possible that Ed Chapman had guessed he would come riding into Saddlerock, even though there was a posse out scouring the countryside for him, and if so, he and the two others would have his route marked out by now, through the dark streets, knowing he would come looking for them, and they would know all of the safe and dark places in town where they could set an ambush for him without much danger to themselves. He supposed, from what he knew of the lay-out of Saddlerock, the most likely place would be somewhere between the main hotel and the far end of the street, but perhaps for that very reason they would not use that place, but get him even before he reached the square.

His alertness was sharp now, the hot black coffee seemed to have sharpened his senses to a remarkable degree, washing away all of the weariness that had been in him from the moment he had ridden into town. Silence lay along the dark boardwalk as he strode along, eyes flicking from one side of the street to the other. He saw a couple of dim shadows cross the street twenty yards in front of him, just at the edge of the square, saw them pause and turn, peering back in his direction. Then one of the men caught at his companion's arm, pulled him along, back on to the other boardwalk and out of sight around the corner.

Two of the Chapman gang? The thought flicked through his mind, then he dismissed it instantly. If they had been, they would have sent shots in his direction by now. He paused for a moment, undecided as to his next move, then continued on towards the square. At the edge of the boardwalk he paused. He was like an animal now. He could sense danger in town, lurking in the shadows, but he could see nothing. A drunk staggered down the steps of one of the saloons, the yellow light shining at his back for a moment as the doors swung open, holding his swaying figure silhouetted against the glare. Then the doors snapped shut and the man reached the dusty street and moved slowly and haltingly along it, feet shuffling in the dust. Matt watched him go, then snapped his attention around, hand streaking for the gun at his waist as a voice reached him from the shadows.

A second later he knew that if the voice had belonged to one of his enemies he would have been dead by now.

'Careful, Turner!' The dark shadow could just be seen, paused in a narrow opening between two of the buildings. Matt tried to make out the other's face but could see nothing under the wide-brimmed hat.

'Who's that?' he hissed, holding the Colt, balanced in the palm of his right hand, finger laid across the smooth steel of the trigger.

'Doc Parsons. I recognised you in the hotel a few minutes back, guessed why you're here.'

Matt moved forward, still alert, then relaxed a little as he recognised the little sawbones. He pouched his gun, knowing there was no immediate danger here.

'You got something on your mind, Doc?' he asked thickly, throwing a quick glance along the street in both directions. 'Why didn't you just shoot me in the back and claim that thousand dollrs reward?'

Parsons shook his head slowly. 'Reckon you know me better than that,' he said thinly. 'Besides, I saw Ed Chapman ride into town a while back. You don't have to be a Pinkerton man to know he fits into this deal.'

'He was the leader of that gang that

robbed the stage and killed those men,' murmured Matt hoarsely.

The other nodded. 'I know. I reckon Sheriff Hogan knows, too, but there's no proof. They framed you real good for that job. The warrant is still out for your arrest on a charge of robbery and murder.'

'I figured that,' said Matt with a trace of bitterness to his voice. 'That's why I came back to town. I've been trailing Chapman all the way from Tucson. I got his brother there, nearly got him. I suppose he's linked up with those other two coyotes.'

'That's right. When I saw you moving out of the hotel and in this direction, I figured you might need a little information.'

'So you know where they are right now?' This was more than Matt had hoped for.

'Over in the Trail's End saloon.'

'Where's that?'

'Near the end of the main street, a couple of hundred yards past the sheriff's office. Down by the warehouses.'

'I know,' Matt nodded tersely. 'Thanks for the information, Doc.' He glanced down and saw to his surprise that the other had strapped on a gunbelt. His eyes widened a little, then he said, tight-lipped: 'Why're you carrying a gun, Doc? You ain't figuring on coming with me, are you?'

'I figured you might need a little help,' admitted the other. 'Long time since I used a gun against any of my fellow-men, always found a knife and scalpel a little more effective so far, but I guess there can be times when you have to use other instruments to get rid of rattlers like these.'

Matt shook his head vehemently, and caught hold of the other's arm. 'No, Doc,' he said decisively. 'Time was when I might have been glad of your help. But this fight is no concern of yours. Don't get me wrong about this, but you'd make it more difficult for me.'

'You trying to say I'd be in the way?' protested the other, indignantly.

'Not exactly, but I'd always have the feeling I'd need to keep an eye on you. These men are killers, Doc. They're men who know how to handle guns and they won't hesitate to put a slug into you, no matter who you are. I figure you might hesitate just that fraction of a second before pulling the trigger. You ain't a born killer, Doc, that's what it amounts to — and when you're facing up to polecats like these, you have to be.'

Parsons ran his fingers over the guns in his belt, lips tight, a curious expression on his face. Then he nodded slowly. 'Mebbe you're right,' he acknowledged reluctantly. 'But be careful. They know you're heading into town after 'em. I heard them talking a while ago. They're going to split up and take you when you arrive.'

Matt smiled grimly. 'I've been in town for the best part of a couple of

221

hours now and they ain't found me,' he muttered. He lifted his head and stared sombrely in the direction of the square. 'The Trail's End, you say. Guess it's time I paid 'em a call. No sense in keeping men like that waiting, is there?'

Parsons looked up. 'You determined to go after those three alone? Do you want to get yourself killed? You're a target for any one of them the minute you step out into that street yonder. And there are plenty of townsfolk who still reckon you were in that gang. Any man with an itchy trigger finger and a yen for a thousand dollars will be ready to jump you.'

Matt grinned sourly. 'You got any other suggestion to make as to how I can get 'em? No point in skulkin' along alleys waiting for 'em to come to me. Or do you reckon I ought to ride out and keep on riding, having to live with this for the rest of my life?'

'Depends on whether you want to stay alive,' said the other.

'Sure I want to stay alive, believe me,'

Matt paused, and then went on: 'You know as well as I do that an ambusher is a coward, a man who's afraid to face up to a man and give him an equal chance. And it's always easier for a bushwhacker to kill a man who's scared. I just don't aim to make it easy for anybody, that's all.'

'Then if you're determined to go through with it, make sure they don't shoot you in the back.' Parsons studied his face in the dim light, leaning forward a little. Then, shaking his head slightly, he turned on his heel and made his way back into the shadows of the narrow alley.

The street seemed quiet. A couple of men rode out of town and the dust of their passing settled slowly in the dimness. It was only possible to make out anything where the streams of light from the windows lanced across the darkness. Ten minutes later he stood on the boardwalk and eyed the entrance to the Trail's End saloon on the opposite side of the street. The sound of a tinny

223

piano came from it, reaching his ears above the lusty yelling of the men as they sang one of the old southern songs at the tops of their voices, most of them off-key and out of tune.

The sleeping anger woke in him afresh as he stood there, every nerve and muscle in his body tight with the growing tension. He lifted the guns in their holsters a little, easing them up and down in the leather, then dropped them back, made up his mind and strode over to the saloon, thrusting open the doors and stepping inside, the sense of time being wasted pushing him on.

There were four men playing poker at one of the tables and a small man in a brightly coloured jacket playing the piano in the corner of the room. A couple of men were standing with their elbows on the top of the piano, singing loudly but, apart from them, and the bartender at the back of the bar, the place was empty.

Cautiously, puzzled, Matt swung his

gaze around the room, then stepped over to the bar. The barkeep came up, stood eyeing him for a moment.

'Whisky!' said Matt harshly.

The other reached behind the counter, brought up a glass and a half-empty bottle and set them in front of him, then eased himself away. Matt watched him out of the corner of his eye, then said softly: 'You don't seem to be busy tonight.'

'Most of the boys are out of town with the sheriff. Word came this afternoon that they've got one of those hombres who held up the stage trapped at the McEwen ranch about fifteen miles east of here.'

Matt pursed his lips and shrugged negligently. 'You reckon they'll get him?'

'If he's still there when the posse arrives, there ain't any doubt about it,' he declared.

'What about the other men who were with him when the stage was held up?'

'Reckon nobody knows where they're hiding out. Probably they'll be over the border by now, out of reach of the law. If this hombre had any sense, that's where he'd be.'

Matt let his glance slide a little to one side, to the far end of the bar. There was a door there which he had only just noticed. Out of the corner of his eye he had felt certain it had opened just an inch and then been closed quickly, as if somebody had been standing at the back of it, peering through at him. Holding his drink in his left hand, Matt moved rapidly to the end of the bar and, before the bartender could stop him, had thrown open the door. Inside there was a small room with a door leading out into a narrow, rubbish-filled alley. On the table were the remains of a meal and he saw at once three men had been eating there.

The three members of the Chapman gang? Judging from what Doc Parsons had told him, that seemed more than likely. He spun swiftly on his heel, caught the look on the bartender's face and knew he was right in his surmise.

Placing the drink on the small table, he tugged the gun from its holster and went out into the alley, treading softly, eyes switching from one side to the other, alert and expecting trouble. He knew he was an exposed target if any of those men were crouched in the shadows, sighting their weapons on him at this particular moment, fingers tightening on triggers. Waiting was not in him now. He was filled with a savage and desperate sense of urgency. He had travelled too far and too fast to be put off now by any considerations for his own safety.

Crouching low, he hugged the wall of the small saloon, soft-footing it along the alley, the gun in his hand ready for use. At the far end of the narrow passage, the hulk of a tumbledown building loomed up in front of him.

7

Death of an Outlaw

For a moment Matt paused in the shadows. Then he saw a dark shape weave through a dim pattern of yellow light, heard the scuffle of steps as the man ran into the ruined building at a ragged run. Sucking in a deep breath, Matt ran forward, still hugging the saloon wall, casting about him for any sign of the other two men he knew to be somewhere around. He could see nothing of them. That the trio had split up, determined to take him from different sides, was obvious. He tried to guess at their actions. Hesitating, the sound of soft footsteps inside the abandoned house reached him and he went forward, ducked his head as he passed through the low, narrow entrance, pushing himself swiftly to one side. The killer was in front of him now, circling around in the dimness, angling to one side, trying to get into a position where he could put in a killing shot without exposing himself too much.

There was the musty smell of the abandoned house sharp in his nostrils and the dust irritated the back of his throat, making him want to cough, but he knew that the slightest sound would give away his position to the waiting gunman. He held his breath, searching with eyes and ears for anything that would tell him where the other was. Then, faint and far away, he picked up the other's harsh breathing, knew that the long waiting, the silence, had finally forced the other to let the air go from his lungs in that harsh sigh. Swiftly he jerked up the gun, squeezed off a couple of shots. The blooming flash from the muzzle, stabbing out into the pitch blackness, almost blinded him. Dimly he heard the two slugs tear their way through wood and stone. The return fire was almost immediate, the bullets crashing through the spot where he had been standing a few seconds earlier, hitting the wall just above his head after he had dived instinctively to one side. He struck the floor with a blow that sent a stab of agony lancing along his injured shoulder. With an effort he bit down on the cry that sprang unbidden to his lips, lay still for a long moment. He could hear the gunman moving around softly and cautiously, not sure whether either of those slugs had hit him.

Very gently, he crawled forward, holding his breath. He knew there had to be a stairway or the remains of one somewhere in the darkness, because the sounds of the other's feet had come from above him. Somehow, the other had reached the upper storey and was therefore able to fire down at him, to pin him down without the chance of getting much cover from what little furniture was still in the lower room.

Sightlessly he explored in front of him with his left hand, feeling in the dark for something solid which would tell him where he was. For a moment he felt nothing, then his arm struck something hard and tall, making a definite sound in spite of the precautions he was taking. A bullet slammed into the wooden floor near him and, a second later, he realised he had come upon the stairs which led upstairs to where the killer lay crouched in the darkness.

Patience made him crouch there, utterly still, not moving an inch. It was the waiting that soon broke the other man down. He heard the loud, harsh, gusty sigh that came from the man's lips, heard the savagely muttered curse as the other realised this sound had given away his position to the man waiting below. As if realising he had no other choice, the gunman fired swiftly and savagely, moving his guns in a wide arc, hoping to get Matt, to hit him if he fired a sufficiently large number of shots in all directions.

Jerking the gun up, Matt fired one

shot, heard a loud cry go up from the man above him. There was the sound of choking as the breath rattled eerily in the other's throat, then his body fell against the banister railing at the head of the stairs and came tumbling head over heels to the bottom. Matt listened intently, then moved slowly forward when he heard no breathing. His knee touched something soft and yielding and he fumbled over the other's chest, felt his hand come away soft and sticky, caught the curious limpness of the man's arm, fingers utterly relaxed, the gun lying on the floor at his side.

Throwing a swift glance at the open window, he felt in his pocket, struck a sulphur match and held the tiny glowing flame close to the man's face. He recognised the other as one of the men against whom he had testified at the trial in Tucson. It was not Ed Chapman. The other was still some-where around in town, with the last remaining member of the gang.

The match spluttered out against his

fingers and he dropped it on to the floor, rising slowly to his feet. There was still a dull ache in his right shoulder and for a moment he thought he had opened the wound. A swift examination told him this was not so, but he knew the odds were still weighted against him. These other two men would have heard the shooting by now and would be ready for him if they saw that he emerged alive.

Going to the splintered doorway, he paused for a moment well back in the shadows, peering out. Nothing moved in the alley, no sign of the other two gunmen.

★ ★ ★

The sound of running feet broke the clinging stillness, shattering it like the racket of gunfire that had preceded it. Backing away, he crushed through the narrow space between the ruined house and that which stood next to it, moving back into the deep shadows where he could not be seen. The bartender from the saloon came running into view first. He was followed by several other men who stood in a small knot for a moment, staring about them.

'I'd swear those shots came from in there,' called one of the men. Matt saw him point towards the dark building.

'Reckon it'd be that hombre who came in ten minutes ago,' shouted the barkeep. He suddenly thrust his way to the forefront of the small group. 'He seemed interested in how busy we were, then pushed his way out through the room and into the alley. He had his gun in his hand when he ran out.'

Matt smiled grimly to himself in the darkness. So far, none of the men seemed anxious to go inside the building and see what had happened. He guessed they were still a little apprehensive, did not wish to expose themselves to any gunfire that might break out at any moment. Finally, they overcame their distrust of the stillness in the dark building and several pushed their way inside, the bartender remaining in the alley, easily seen by his white apron.

There was a moment's silence. Then two men came out of the splintered doorway and one of them said: 'There's a dead hombre in there, Tom. Better get the sheriff over right away and — no, dammit, Hogan's out with the posse. We'll have to wait until he gets back.'

'Any use sending for Doc Parsons?'

'Nope, he's dead, shot through the chest. It don't look like the man who ran out of the saloon.'

'Then he must be the killer. He can't have got far. If we spread out and search for him, we ought to pick him up before long.'

'Might be best if we was to wait for the sheriff,' cautioned the other hesitantly. 'He's armed and he's shown he won't hesitate to kill. Don't figure any of us ought to step up against him. The law should be back any minute.'

One by one the other men came out of the house and stood in the yard, looking at each other. It was apparent most of them were of the same mind; this was really none of their business, they ought to wait for the sheriff and the posse to get back to town and inform him, leave it up to him to catch the killer. None of them seemed to be of the opinion it might have been a fair fight, even though they must have spotted the gun near the outlaw's body, a gun which had obviously been used.

The men stood around for several minutes talking. Then they began to drift away in ones and twos. The bartender was one of the last to go. He stood there in the dimness, staring about him into the shadows that lay thick and deep in the alley, as if he could pick out Matt by simply looking about him. Then he turned abruptly on his heel and walked back to the saloon, closing the rear door after him.

Matt waited in silence for another three minutes until he was sure none of the men would come back, then slipped out of the shadows and moved soft-footed past the exit of the saloon out into the street. There was a bunch of men gathered on the boardwalk, but they had their backs to him as he emerged from the alley and none of them spotted him as he walked swiftly and silently away, back in the direction of the square.

Inwardly, he wondered how long it would be before Hogan and the posse returned to Saddlerock, after finding they had ridden off on a wild goose chase. There was the chance, of course, they may decide to ride on into Tucson, possibly believing the rancher when he informed them of the direction he had taken when he had ridden out of the ranch. But it was doubtful if a man as wily as Sheriff Hogan would fall for a ruse like that. He was more likely to think Matt would turn and swing back towards Saddlerock, knowing the Chapman gang would be there. In a case such as this, revenge often overrode natural caution.

He moved carefully towards the screening blackness of the large warehouse which stood alone on the side of the street. Not a solitary light showed there, but it afforded plenty of cover, and for anyone moving hurriedly away from the Trail's End saloon, it would provide an excellent hiding place from which to watch events.

Hidden in the darkness, he moved into the shadow of the tall, long building. There was the stink of hides in the air, gagging at the back of his nostrils. The warehouse was a big, hollow-ringing place, with the hides piled high in heaps on either side and narrow passages left between the rows. He searched the place from end to end, moving with caution, his guns in his hands. But there was no sign of anyone there and in the end he was forced to the conclusion that Ed Chapman and his companion had left hurriedly once they knew he was alive and it was their companion who had been shot dead.

He sucked in his lips sharply,

undecided as to his next move. He wanted to move out and make his way along to the square, to search there for the two men he had to find, but he knew that to do this would be putting himself in great danger. The citizens of Saddlerock would have been alerted by now, would have heard that shooting and knew what it meant.

The sense of time pressing him into action was strong within him. He knew he had very little time left in which to locate Ed Chapman and his companion. Once the sheriff got back with his men, it would be only a matter of time before he was found. Whether he could talk Hogan and the others into looking out for Chapman and bringing him in for questioning was something he did not know. The trap against him had been laid too well for anyone to believe him, and all of the men he had run into so far were dead and would not be answering any questions put to them by the law.

He reached a sudden decision,

stepped into one of the alleys, cut across a couple of vacant plots of ground, past a tin-can dump and then along one of the narrow streets. Halfway along he found the place he was looking for. There was a pale yellow light shining out of the window and, glancing in, he saw the short figure of Doc Parsons seated in the high-backed chair in front of the fire.

Knocking softly on the door, he waited. For a moment there was no sign that the other had heard his knock, then he heard shuffling at the other side of the door and a second later it creaked open and the sawbones stood in the opening. Parsons threw a quick glance in all directions, then pulled him inside, shutting the door behind him.

'You all right?' he asked tightly. 'I heard shooting a while ago and guessed it might be you. It came from the right direction of town. Did you find those men?'

Matt sank down in one of the chairs in the small room while the other closed the wooden shutters over the windows. He nodded wearily. 'I got a smell of 'em at the Trail's End, but they slipped out of the back, must've seen me walk in, and there they split up. I caught up with one of 'em in an empty house at the back of the saloon.'

Doc Parsons lifted thick, grey brows. 'He's dead now?'

'That's right. No need for you to go out there, Doc. Pity is that he didn't talk before he died. It might have made things a lot easier. As it is, I've no idea where the other two men are at this moment. They could be anywhere in Saddlerock, I guess. May even have saddled up and ridden out, knowing Hogan and his posse might be back in town before midnight.'

'That's more than likely,' nodded the other. He sat down in the high-backed chair and regarded Matt seriously. 'What do you intend to do now? You don't have much time to do anything, I reckon. Once Hogan gets back he'll have to come looking for you, no matter what he thinks himself.'

Matt leaned forward. 'If you were in Chapman's place and you wanted to make sure you killed a man without running much risk of being shot down yourself, where in Saddlerock would you set up an ambush?'

The other drew the thick, grey brows together in a tight line. 'There ain't many places,' he said finally, forehead wrinkled in thought. 'There's the warehouse back along the main street.'

'I've been there, searched it from one end to the other. No sign of either of 'em there.'

'There aren't many other places that fit the bill.' He glanced up at Matt. 'Why don't you wait until Hogan gets back, give yourself up and tell him all you've told me?'

Matt laughed harshly and bitterly. 'You reckon I'd even get that chance? They'd shoot me down as soon as they saw me. Mebbe not the sheriff but the others. They're still convinced I was the leader of that band. Nothing I'm able to say will change their minds about that.'

'You want me to put in a word for you?' inquired the other. 'I reckon I still have some say in matters here.'

Matt hesitated, mulling that over in his mind. It seemed an easy way out, but eventually he shook his head. 'Nope, Doc, it wouldn't work and I don't want to involve anybody else in this. Too many people have been hurt or killed because of it.' He spoke with a deep weariness in his tone. 'I wonder why such a thing should happen to me, something that seems to have changed me completely. Do you know, Doc, I've killed God knows how many men since I pulled out of town just a short while ago, something I'd never have done before.'

'When a man is framed as you were, he has to change. If he tries to run, it doesn't do him any good,' said the other musingly. 'He can only run so far and then he finds himself out of steam. And you don't reckon those outlaws would have left you alone once they discovered you'd been let out of jail by the sheriff, do you? They only framed you for one thing. Not to throw suspicion from them, but to make certain you'd be destroyed. When they found out you hadn't been lynched by the mob, they'd keep after you until they'd made certain themselves.'

There was a good deal of truth in what the old man said, Matt reflected. He had been forced into these ways of violence by circumstances and not from choice. But how many other outlaws and killers could look back on their lives and say the same thing? That was the frightening thing about the whole business. Where would it all end for him? Would he be able to hang up his gun once these two men had been killed or brought to justice? Or would there be more killing, murder without an end until he was shot down himself? Would they point him out as the man who took on the entire Chapman gang single-handed and licked them all, a target for any trigger-happy young gunman who decided to try his luck against the great Matt Turner, gunslick and killer?

He hoped with all his heart this would never happen. He told himself, sitting there opposite old Doc Parsons, he would sooner be shot dead by Ed Chapman than that should happen to him.

The other seemed to tell from the expression on his face what kind of thoughts were running through his mind at that moment for he said quietly: 'A man has to do what he thinks is right, Matt. Even if at the time it seems to everyone that he's acting against the law. You have to live with your conscience for the rest of your life and somehow I doubt if you could do that if you back down now.'

'I'm glad there's somebody who sees it that way.' Matt sighed and forced himself to relax a little. 'As men go, this gang is at the bottom of the pile.'

Doc Parsons nodded slowly, eyes serious, the lids drawn well down over them. He seemed to be debating within himself. For a moment, he sat absolutely still, then opened his mouth to say something, but it was never said for at that precise moment there was the sound of drumming hooves in the distant main street. Swiftly Matt rose to his feet and walked over to the shuttered window, motioning to the other to douse the lamp. Cupping his hand over the glass, Parsons extinguished the lamp on the table, and in the warm darkness Matt pulled aside one of the shutters and peered out. From the window he could just make out the square standing at the far end of the narrow street. There was a flood of light there from the windows of the hotel and saloons. He waited and a few moments later saw the bunch of close-packed riders move past his vision.

'The sheriff and his posse back?' said Parsons, in a soft voice. It was more of a statement than a question.

Bitterly, Matt nodded. He turned,

sliding the shutter across into place. Doc Parsons lit the lamp again, the yellow glow flooding to every corner of the room. He looked appraisingly at Matt over the table.

'You can't go out looking for those men now,' he said decisively. 'The posse will nail you before you can ever hope to locate them. Better hide up here until the morning. I'll make discreet inquiries about them.'

Matt opened his mouth to protest at the other's plan. He felt he was so close to what he had set out to do that there was no time to waste. And by the morning there was the possibility that the two men would have left town, considering it to be too hot for them with the sheriff back. But he forced the protest down. The other had a point there. If the two men remained watching all night for him, without finding him, without even the posse finding him, they might relax their vigilance by morning and make his task easier.

Besides, there was a deep-seated weariness in his body which made his brain move sluggishly and the riot of ideas in his mind did not make for quick thinking.

'You're right, Doc,' he said firmly. 'But what do we do if the posse decide to make a search tonight?'

'If they should decide to come here they'll never find you,' said the other firmly. 'Besides, why should they suspect me of hiding an outlaw and a killer?'

* * *

Gratefully, Matt sank down on the bare boards flooring the loft of the house and stretched himself out to his fullest extent, grateful for the rest and the chance to do a little thinking. So far, he had been on the run to clear himself of the law and to track down the men who had framed him with the robbery and murder and who themselves sought his death. All he wished now was a straight chance at the two men he still sought, an even encounter with them. He knew he wanted nothing more and would be content with nothing less. After all he had been through, fate owed that much to him. It was another deep obligation in his life, something he had to see through or die in the attempt, otherwise he would never be able to lift his face again, would never be able to walk without fear and with dignity among his fellow men.

He turned slightly on the hard boards, listening intently to the faint sounds in the distance, sounds of the town muffled by the thick walls. For some odd reason his mind kept turning back to the memory of a tall, slender girl who had helped him, nursing him back to health after he had been shot in the shoulder, believing in him in spite of everything. Rosaria Lynd who had made him promise to ride back that way when all this was over and finished.

Would he keep that promise if he were alive to do so? He wondered vaguely. Or was that simply another episode in his life which was best forgotten? What had a man like Matt Turner to offer a girl like that?

He felt a surge of bitterness pass through him. A hunted criminal, trying to keep one jump ahead of the law. A man who rode with bitter knowledge that he had shot down several of his fellow men, and even the knowledge it had been fair fight and they had been outlaws, men who deserved killing, seemed to make little difference to him at that moment. Perhaps, in time, the feeling would wear off, become tempered by other events.

There was the sound of shouting somewhere in the distance. For a moment, he sat upright in his blankets, trying to place the sound, but it was impossible to tell whether it was coming closer or receding. Lying back, he tried to compose his thoughts. It was relatively easy to relax his body, but when a man was troubled by such thoughts as haunted him, how did he relax his mind?

Clasping his hands at the back of his neck, he stared up at the low ceiling over his head. How long he lay there, lost in thought, it was impossible for him to tell. He was jerked rudely back to the present by a loud knocking on the street door down below. Someone yelled something at the top of his voice and a moment fled before he recognised the harsh tones of Chet Wainwright, the man who had been so anxious to see him strung up when he had last been in Saddlerock.

A pause and then there was the sound of Doc's shuffling footsteps moving towards the door. It creaked open and Matt could hear every word that was said down below.

Wainwright's tones called: 'We're looking for that hombre Turner, who held up the stage a while back, Doc. We've got reason to believe he's in town right now. He was seen by the bartender at the Trail's End just before a man was killed in the old Thomson place nearby.'

'I ain't seen no strangers around town this evening,' muttered Doc Parsons quietly. 'Why come here at this time of night?'

'Got to make sure he ain't hiding any place,' said the other. 'Sheriff's got some men and they're checking the saloons and hotels. Once we've finished along here we'll check with the livery stables. If he did ride into town, I figure his horse will be somewhere around. Then we'll know for sure that he's still here.'

'Mind if we step inside and take a look around the place, Doc?' called another voice Matt did not recognise.

'Now hold on a minute,' said Doc protestingly. 'I ain't going to have — '

'We can always get the sheriff over,' said Wainwright, and there was an ominous undertone to his voice. 'We ain't suggestin' for one minute that you're hiding him, Doc, but he may have been hit during the gunfight and you'd be the first person he'd come to to patch him.'

'Well, there ain't been nobody here all night,' said the other thinly. 'But if you got to come in and look the place over, come inside.'

Matt lay tensely on the hard floor, listening to the men as they came into the house. He could hear them moving around downstairs, shifting pieces of furniture around, talking softly among themselves. Once he heard someone pause directly below the spot where he was lying. Wainwright's voice, seemingly less than two feet below him, asked: 'Where does that lead to, Doc?'

'Nowhere special. Out on to the roof of the building if you must know. If you figure he went up there, then he'll have ridden out of town by now.'

'All right.' A pause, then the other called: 'Found anything suspicious here, boys?'

'Nothing here. Reckon he can't have come as far as this.'

'Well, he's around somewhere. Ed,

you'd better check on the livery stables. Ain't likely he left his mount at Thorpe's, check the others first. If his sorrel is there, get back and let us know.'

Matt heard one of the men go out into the street. His hurrying footsteps faded swiftly into the distance. It would not be long before they discovered where the sorrel had been stabled and although the livery man would not have seen his face, he would have remembered the man who had brought the horse in, had deliberately kept his face in the shadow as if he had something to hide and did not want to be recognised. As he lay there, forcing himself to breathe slowly, he realised the trap was closing in on him rapidly. Soon, unless he did something about it, he would become enmeshed in it, unable to move.

'If you should get a visit from him during the night, remember there's a thousand dollars for him, dead or alive.' Wainwright spoke quickly to Doc

Parsons as they pulled out in the street.

'I'll remember,' said Doc quietly.

Now the immediate danger was past, Matt lay back in his blankets and closed his eyes, but sleep was long in coming, and when it did he fell into an uneasy doze from which he woke unrefreshed, with the heat beginning to burn the air in the small loft, telling him, although he could not see it for himself, that the sun was already up.

Doc Parsons must have heard him stirring for a few moments later there was a sharp rap on the wooden trapdoor set in the floor of the loft, and Doc's voice reached him from below: 'It's safe to come down now, Matt,' he shouted, raising his voice a little in order to make himself heard through the thick wood.

Matt got to his feet, prised up the trapdoor and lowered himself down into the room below. Old Doc turned and grinned at him broadly. 'Reckon you'd hear 'em when they came last night. I soon sent 'em packing.'

'D'you know if they found my horse?'

'Heard nothing, but if you left it at one of the stables, I don't see how they could have missed it. They'll know you're in town.'

'Not much doubt about that.' Matt followed the other into the small parlour. Doc had fried some bacon and eggs and there was the rich smell of coffee in the pot.

'Once you've eaten you'd better lie low while I go out and find out what's happened,' murmured the other. 'They will still be looking for you, but if I can find out where those two men are you're looking for, you might be able to get to them before Wainwright and the others get you.'

After Doc Parsons had left, Matt moved across the room and took up a position by the window looking out on to the street, watching the folk who passed by. The sun beat down on everything, laying a scorching finger on the dusty street and the glistening roofs of the small houses. It promised to be another unpleasantly hot day in this hell-hole of a town, he reflected bitterly.

His fingers tightened savagely on the back of the chair in front of him. This was a part of the business he didn't like. Waiting for something to break, not knowing when nor where it would come to meet him; waiting while another man went out and faced whatever danger might be lurking out there in the streets of Saddlerock, for he had no doubts whatever in his mind that if Doc Parsons wasn't too careful, he might give himself away, asking his pointed questions; and he knew that Ed Chapman would be in no mood to hold off shooting down a man like Doc Parsons if he once suspected the other was trying to shield him, and knew where he could be found.

The minutes dragged. Outside the heat head increased in its piled up intensity. A small group of riders dusted by, riding their mounts slowly. They looked to the right and left as they passed and his eyes narrowed just a shade as he noticed the long-barrelled rifles some of them carried in their right hands. More men out looking for him, he decided. He watched closely until they swung away, out of sight around the corner of the street. His body was tense, his eyes hard and glittering, and his disposition at that moment was about as edgy as that of a tormented rattler.

The knowledge that Chapman and the last member of the gang were still somewhere in town, might even have joined forces with these citizens who were hunting him down, brought a savage rush of fury to his mind. He had to pause and fight for control of himself to allow that fury to cool and his hands to steady on the back of the chair.

Doc Parsons returned half an hour later. He opened the door quickly, hesitated for a moment after glancing speculatively about him, then stepped inside and closed the door behind him. He gave Matt a swift, searching glance that told him nothing and then seated himself at the small table, not speaking for a long moment.

'Well?' demanded Matt harshly, after a brief pause. 'What did you find out about them — if anything?'

'Not much about Chapman — he seems to have gone to earth; but plenty about what's going on in town.'

'I ain't interested overmuch in the rest of the town,' grunted Matt thickly. The anger and the sense of urgency were still in him, deep but bubbling to the surface where he doubted if he would be able to fully control them.

'This is getting to be one hell of a town, Matt,' said the other, almost as if he had not heard the interruption. 'I've lived here for over thirty-five years now. I've watched it grow from a collection of rude, wooden shacks and a solitary saloon into what it is now. I never figured I'd live to see the day when ordinary, decent-living citizens men and women, could become so changed in their ideas that they'd hunt down an innocent man like a hounded animal.'

'You're blaming them just because they're out to kill me?' Matt looked at the other in surprise.

'That's right. I can understand their feelings partly. After all, four men have been killed and three of them had wives and families. But the folk here don't seem able to listen to reason now. This town had a reputation for sheltering wild ones and we know there are still some up there in the hills, and every so often they come down into town. But if the townsfolk only stopped to think, they might see what's happening here. Then they'd realise what sort of men Ed Chapman and the others really are.'

'They know I shot down Chapman's brother and those other men?'

'Sure. They heard all that. Clayburn was a known killer but they figure you had a quarrel over the share-out of the loot and you shot him down.'

Matt tightened his lips into a hard line. It was becoming a very complicated business. How in God's name could the facts become so twisted and distorted in men's minds that anything like this could possibly happen?

A man forced to kill to save his own skin, trapped by a set of circumstances which were not of his own making. It made little sense to him. Outlaws riding openly into town, the very men who had held up that stage and killed the driver and those three deputies, probably riding side by side with the law at that very moment, hunting down an innocent man. He shook his head slowly and sank down into a chair at the other end of the table, facing Parsons. He felt like a piece of timber that had been left out in the desert sun too long, brittle and warped, not able to figure out things straight any longer.

'I understand how you feel,' said the other quietly, not watching him now but staring out through the window. 'Like I said, this is one hell of a town now. But you've got to look at things their way, too. They have their point of view as well, even though it may seem twisted and biased. Those outlaws were mighty clever. They framed you real good for that hold-up and what helped them more than anything was Chet Wainwright being convinced that you were the killer.'

Matt looked up quickly. A sudden thought struck him. 'That's right,' he murmured softly. 'Where does he fit into all this? He seemed damned anxious to get me strung up that night when the mob came hammering on the doors of the jail. If he'd had his way I'd have been dangling at the end of a rope before dawn and without the chance of a proper trial. Seems he's been doing one hell of a lot of talking around town about me.'

'What you got on your mind, Matt?' inquired the other, sitting forward on the edge of his chair.

Matt's eyes were narrowed to mere slits and his fingers were curled a little in front of him. He said: 'You figure he might have some reason for wanting to see me dead, Doc?'

8

Trigger of Hate

Doc Parsons sat silent for a long while, thinking over Matt's question. Then he shrugged his stooped shoulders a little. 'I've known Chet for a long time. He doesn't strike me as the kind of man to get mixed in with Chapman and his crowd, even for a part of the loot.'

He gave Matt another over-bright glance, speculating on him, as if trying to decide the reasoning behind the question. 'He's a pushing man, I'll say that much about him. Somethin's driving him right now but I don't know what it is.' He paused, went on: 'You sure you've never met up with Wainwright before some place? He's a hard character and if he figured he had a grudge against any man he'd never forget it.'

'The face and the name mean nothing to me.' Matt tried to think of where he might have seen the other before he had ridden into Saddlerock from back east, but although he searched his memory, he found nothing there to give him a lead.

Slowly, he said: 'One thing, Doc, if there is any tie-up between Wainwright and these critters, they may be shacking up with him right now. You reckon that makes any kind of sense?'

Doc Parsons still had Matt's earlier question in his mind. 'Could be, I suppose — always assuming that he is tied-in with them.'

Matt rose stiffly to his feet. 'Where can I find this man Wainwright?' There was a distinctly tight edge to his voice now, his eyes fixed on the other. The steely glitter in them told Doc Parsons it would be utterly useless to try to argue with the man who stood in front of him. For a moment he sat there with his hands spread flat on the top of the table. Then he forced himself visibly to relax. 'I hope you know what you're doing, what you're up against.'

'I can guess,' said Matt thinly. 'But they started all of this, and I aim to finish it for 'em. And not even the sheriff and the whole of this town is going to stop me now. If they want trouble, then by God they're going to get it.'

For a moment his tight anger had control over him. He fought it down with an effort, teeth gritted tightly in his mouth so that the muscles of his jaw were lumped painfully under the skin.

'If you're determined to go through with it, and I can see that you are — then you'll find Wainwright next door to the Bank on the main street. But if you go out now in broad daylight they'll pick you up long before you get there. The whole town is crawling with men looking for you. You'd never make it.'

Matt threw a swift glance up at the sky, just visible through the window, then shook his head. 'Too long to wait until dark. I've got to make it now. Besides, this is the time when they'll not be expecting me to appear on the streets. I'll keep an eye open, make my way there through the back alleys. With luck, I ought to get there without too much trouble.'

The other regarded him doubtfully, then scraped back his chair, nodded slowly. 'Keep your eyes peeled. They won't hesitate to shoot you in the back.'

Matt nodded, checked the guns in his belt, then opened the door and glanced out into the bright sunlight that flooded along the street. There were a couple of men at the far end, near the intersection with the main street. They had their backs to him for the moment and he hurried across to the other side, melting into the shadowed boardwalk, keeping his body pressed in tightly against the wooden wall of the building.

He continued with a back line, moving along narrow passages between the houses, in places so narrow that he could barely squeeze through the rough wood, tearing and splintering his hands as he edged forward. He came to a small yard at the rear of the bank building. There was no one around and everything seemed quiet, ominously so. Was he walking into a trap now, he wondered? He eyed the windows at the back of the bank and along the two houses which stood on either side, looking for the barrel of a rifle thrust in his direction with a finger already tightening convulsively on the trigger, but there was nothing like that. As far as he could see, his arrival there had been unnoticed.

For a moment he stood there in the shadows, listening. He could hear horsemen beating steadily through the town and there was the quick hark of voices calling to each other in the distance. As yet they did not seem to be moving in his direction and he began to breathe a little easier. If he did manage to catch up with those two killers he did not want to be disturbed until he had finished what he had set out to do.

Very cautiously he approached the house at the side of the bank where Doc Parsons had told him he could find Wainwright. As he drew closer he eased one of the Colts from its holster, held it loosely in his hand, thumb on the hammer. The door at the rear of the house stood open. Through it he could see nothing.

Tightening his grip on the gun, he paused, then threw himself inside the opening, pressing close to the wall, eyes swiftly adjusting to the gloom, swinging the revolver slowly to cover any movement. The room was a small kitchen and it was empty. There was a pile of crockery in the sink and dust lay everywhere. Not the sort of place he had expected of Chet Wainwright, but there was no telling what kind of man the other really was. A loud-mouthed braggart possibly, but even so, he was also dangerous.

He moved to the far side of the kitchen, treading softly and warily, reached the closed door that opened out of the room, turned the knob in his left hand, then opened it. As he had suspected, it opened directly into the other room on the lower floor of the house. From where he stood he could just make out the figure of the man seated in the high-backed chair, his back to him. For a moment he thought the other was asleep, then the man moved, stretched his arms over his head and got to his feet, moving towards the window, where he paused, dug deep into the pocket of his shirt and came up with a tobacco pouch and proceeded to build himself a smoke, totally oblivious of Matt's presence there.

It was Chet Wainwright. Matt saw the other's features clearly as he half turned, and it would have been the easiest thing in the world to shoot the other down there and then without giving him a chance to defend himself. But he let the chance slide. Instead, he stepped through into the room, saw the startled look of recognition come into the man's eyes. Then the other's hand darted down towards the gun he wore.

'Try it,' snapped Matt. He moved forward a couple of paces further into the room and his eyes never left the other's face. It was always possible to tell whether a man intended to make a play for his guns. The strained look on Wainwright's face suddenly slackened as he realised that Matt had the drop on him and was just waiting for the chance to pull the trigger. With an effort which showed in the beading of sweat that popped out on his forehead, he spread his hands wide, keeping them well away from his belt.

'I guess you've had a hell of a lot more experience in gun play than I have, Turner,' he said, lips compressed into a savage line. His eyes never wavered from Matt's face as if trying to divine the other's intentions. 'I'd be a doggoned fool to walk into that, wouldn't I? You'd shoot me down without any hesitation and I'd never stand a chance.' The thin lips curled disdainfully and he went on slowly, clearly playing for time. 'Just why have you come here, killer? Looking for somebody else to kill?'

Matt shook his head very slowly, deliberately. 'I figure that you might be in cahoots with the real killers, Wainwright. You seemed mighty anxious to have me strung up that night the sheriff arrested me and threw me into jail. Seems to me you couldn't wait for the circuit judge to come around and give me a chance to speak in my own defence.'

'I don't know what you're talking about,' snapped the other, but his eyes were wary now, and there seemed to be a bleak look on his face. 'You trying to say that I've thrown in my lot with some killers?'

'You know damned well what I'm saying. I say that the only reason you wanted me strung up that night, why you headed the posse riding after me into the hills, was because you know who those men were who held up that stage, you knew that it was Ed

Chapman and his gang of killers, and that I was no part of their band.'

'You're lying!' The sharp glitter died slowly from his eyes and he seemed tensed and indrawn. He looked like a man who had been suddenly hollowed out, leaving only an empty shell with no feeling left in him.

'Am I? You know as well as I do that Ed Chapman and another of his killers is here in town. They've been here for a couple of days now, ever since I flushed two of 'em out in Tucson and shot down Ed's brother there.'

Strain suddenly narrowed the other man's face. He looked white under the tan, keyed up, giving full weight of his thoughts to what Matt said. 'If what you say is true, then why don't you go see the sheriff, tell him this? Why come to me with your story?'

'The answer to that is easy.' Matt moved forward another pace, stood with only the table between them. 'Because you know where those two killers are hiding right now. You're keeping them under cover until it's safe for them to go looking for me again.'

'You're wrong.' The other protested his innocence vehemently. He stepped forward, hands outspread. 'I don't know anything about this man Chapman and his — '

Too late, Matt saw that the other did not mean to complete his sentence, that the move he had made had been merely a feint to cover his real intentions. All the time he had been standing there his scheming brain had been thinking ahead. Before Matt knew what was happening, the other dropped his hands, caught the edge of the table and heaved it up with a savage surge of almost super-human strength. The table struck Matt in the middle of the body, hurled him back off balance, the gun slipping from his fingers as he fought to remain upright. He half thought, even as he was falling, that the other would try to go for his guns or run for the door. But instead, Wainwright did a strange and unpredictable thing. He hurled himself bodily over the table, caught Matt around the shoulders and bore him back on to the floor, all of his weight thrusting down heavily on to Matt's chest, knocking the wind from his heaving lungs.

The blow went roaring up through Matt's body and into his brain. He tried to twist to one side under the other's weight, squirming violently, kicking up with his legs as he did so. He felt his knees catch the other in the pit of the stomach, knocking him to one side. A faint whimper of agony came from the other's lips as he rolled a little to one side, giving Matt the chance to free one arm. Wainwright caught hard on his shoulder blades, gave another grunt of pain, then reached down, not to the guns in his belt, but beneath his arm where he must have had another holster. The small pistol he brought out, clutched in his hand, looked tiny and innocent, but there was a grim purpose written on his face as he tried desperately to line the short barrel on

Matt's chest, his finger bar-straight on the trigger.

Desperately Matt caught at the other's wrist, bearing back with all of his strength. Once the other succeeded in lining up that gun, it would mean the end of him, he had no illusions on that score. There was still a dull ringing in his skull, but slowly, inexorably, he forced the other's arm back, bending the wrist with all of his strength. Moments later the inevitable happened. There was a dull crack, the pistol fell from the man's nerveless fingers and he emitted a harsh, shrill scream of pure animal pain and terror. His left hand hung limp where the wrist had been broken.

Sucking air into his lungs, Matt felt the savage anger growing in him now, a deep hatred for the man in front of him and everything that he stood for. At least, he thought with a detached part of his mind, men like Ed Chapman made no secret of the fact that they were gunmen and killers. But with men such as Wainwright, he pretended to be a solid, decent citizen of Saddlerock, while at the same time he was as bad as Chapman and the others.

He thrust himself upward on to his feet and stood there, the table lying on its side a few feet away. He stood and waited while he was able to focus his gaze on the man half lying at his feet on the floor. Gradually the ringing in his head went away and he was able to see clearly again. Wainwright lay moaning softly on the floor, trying to push himself up on to his hands and knees, yet unable to use his left hand. The muscles of his face seemed to have loosened and there was a slackness about his face as he knelt there, scarcely knowing where he was, or what had happened.

'Get up, Wainwright,' muttered Matt thinly. 'Get up and take what's coming to you. This is the end of the line as far as you're concerned.'

The other gave no answer, but continued to kneel there, muttering and mumbling under his breath. Then he lifted his head a little and tried to focus his gaze on Matt, shaking his head slowly from side to side.

Matt took his time and drew back his foot, his toe kicking the other in the side of the head. Slowly, almost as if someone had cut the strings holding his body upright, the other collapsed on to his side with a low moan. Matt stood there for an instant, staring down at him, breathing heavily from the exertion. Then he straightened up, took a deep breath, glanced about him for his gun. It lay on the floor a few feet away near the overturned table. He bent to pick it up, froze abruptly with his fingers less than three inches from it as a hard voice at his back, from the direction of the open doorway, said: 'Hold it right there, Turner, or I'll put a bullet in you right now.'

He stiffened sharply, then rose slowly to his full height, turning a little to face the other. The man stood just inside the doorway with the sixer levelled at him.

There was a smile of brutal triumph on the man's face and a harsh glitter at the back of his eyes.

'We figured you might come here, buster,' he said, hoarsely. He let his glance fall for just a moment to where Wainwright lay unconscious on the floor, his arms outflung in front of him. 'Seems I got here just in time. You roughed him up a little, I reckon he'd like to finish this with you, but there ain't time for that. You've been a lot of trouble to us. Ed figures you know too much. That's why you've got to be stopped before you talk with the sheriff. Not that he's likely to believe you, but it could make things awkward for us.'

'So you're the other one who's been working with Chapman.' Matt spoke clearly.

'That's right. You didn't figure you could get away with this all of the time, did you?' The gunman uttered a harsh laugh. 'I'd kill you here and now if it was up to me, but Chapman wants to do that himself. Seems you shot up two

278

of his brothers. He doesn't like that and I reckon before you die you're going to be pleading with him for death.'

The other seemed to be enjoying himself immensely, but not once did the barrel of the gun waver in the other's fist. Matt felt the tightness grow in his chest. Mentally, he estimated his chances of jumping the other, saw the hungry look in the man's eyes, knew that he was only waiting for him to make such a move, to give him the excuse to shoot him down where he stood. The gunman would know that three members of the gang had already met their deaths at Matt's hands and they would be determined not to take any chance with him.

'Reckon you'd better ease that other gun slowly out of its holster and drop it on the floor.'

Matt hesitated, saw from the killing fever in the other's eyes that he meant business, and lowered his hand slowly to the butt of the Colt, gently lifted it clear of leather, held it between his

279

fingers for a moment, then released his hold. The weapon clattered to the floor at his feet. But Matt's gaze was not fixed on the gun but on the man's face in front of him. The other had advanced a little further into the room, obviously believing that there was little danger now that Matt was unarmed. He did just as Matt figured he would. At the moment that he let go of the Colt, dropping it to the floor, the gunman's eyes swung downward, instinctively, to follow it. Scarcely had it hit the floor than he swung round, bunched fist lashing upward at the other's chin. In the same moment, he stepped to one side. Instinctively, the other squeezed down on the trigger in the same moment that he staggered back under the vicious blow which took him completely by surprise. His eyes took on a glassy stare as he slumped back against the wall, the slug from the smoking Colt tearing a furrow in the wooden floor a couple of inches from Matt's right foot. The man was almost out on his feet but he still retained that spark of consciousness, or awareness, that made him hold on to the gun, striving with all of the buckling strength left in him to lift the barrel and line it on Matt's chest.

Forcing himself upright, Matt smashed his fist into the man's unprotected throat. The gunman gurgled with pain and fell back, shoulders hard against the wall as his paralysed neck muscles tried to work, to allow him to suck air down into his starved lungs. Matt followed up his advantage with short, chopping blows to the side of the other's face.

Acting on instinct, the gunslick rolled away, along the wall. He had lost his grip on the Colt now and there was a new expression in his deep-set eyes when he drew himself up to face Matt — fear. He was no longer as sure of himself as he had been a few moments earlier. Now the tables had been turned with a vengeance.

But he was a hard man, tough and

wiry, and he fought with all the dirty tricks he had learned on the way. His eyes narrowed to mere slits as he fought back, came boring in, fingers jabbing for Matt's face as he sought to gouge his eyes from their sockets. Savagely, Matt pulled his head to one side, the jerk almost tearing his head from his shoulders. The other's fingers raked along his cheeks, missing his eyes by less than an inch. Thrusting up with the heel of his hand under the other's chin, he began to exert more force, thrusting the man's head back, jamming it hard against the wall. Grunting savagely, the man was forced to back up, but he was far from finished. He must have realised that unless he did something fast, he was a dead man.

His eyes flickered to one side. Too late, Matt noticed the heavy carved ornament that stood on a small table by the wall. The man's fingers closed on it and a second later he lifted his hand and swung it hard down against the side of Matt's face. The blow struck him just behind the left ear. Pain jarred redly through his skull and there was a dull roaring in his ears that drowned out everything else. A red mist hovered and swayed in front of his vision and he fought savagely to focus his eyes on the other's distorted features as they floated blurringly in front of him.

He felt the weariness that came from the fight with Wainwright descend on his body, dragging at his limbs. For the first time he glimpsed defeat at the hands of the killer. Dropping his right shoulder, ignoring the pain that lanced through it and along his arm, he drove it like a battering ram into the other's chest, felt the man stagger and fall back. A grunt came from the guman's lips as all of the air was driven from his lungs by the shattering blow. Then, without warning, the other rushed forward, arms outspread, throwing them around Matt's waist, bearing him back with his weight, squeezing, his fists clenching tightly in the small of Matt's back, pulling with all of his strength. He felt himself being lifted off his feet as the other continued to exert more pressure, and he knew it could only be a matter of time before his spine reached the limit of the punishment it could take and snapped like a rotten twig. The pain made him feel dizzy. He struggled to free himself, but both of his arms were pinioned to his sides.

Sharply he brought up both knees into the gunman's crotch, felt the pressure around his body slacken fleetingly as the other tried to cover up and protect himself against a second blow. With a desperate surging of strength, Matt managed to get both arms free. Before the other could recover himself, he smashed down with the flats of his palms against the other's skull, just behind the ears. The gunman toppled like a felled tree, stumbled against the wall, then slid down it.

For a long moment, Matt found himself unable to move. He could scarcely see anything through the wavering red mist that danced tantalisingly in front of his eyes. He knew that he had to stop the other now. There was, however, no chance to seek his guns on the floor. He drew back his right foot and kicked the man savagely on the head and chest as he had Wainwright a little while earlier.

He fell forward on to his face, striking the side of his head against the sharply angled corner of the table. He did not move as Matt stepped back, ready for any further trouble. But he knew instinctively as he stood there, drawing air into his lungs in great, rasping gulps, that there would be no more trouble from either of these two men. Wainwright was clearly unconscious and likely to remain so for some time. He did not bother to check whether the gunman was alive or dead. There was only one emotion burning in him now like a leaping flame. The desire to locate Ed Chapman and finish the score with him. He had almost run into a trap here. He did not intend to let that happen a second time and, now that he knew there was only Chapman left to take care of, the grim purpose in his mind outweighed every other consideration.

Bending, he picked up his guns and thrust them deep into the holsters. For a moment he had trouble standing up straight and his knees seemed to be buckling under him as if unable to support his weight. But gradually feeling and strength came back into them and he was able to move towards the door leading out into the street. The two brutal beatings he had taken had left his arms and legs numb and even his brain seemed to have lost a lot of feeling.

As he paused there, hand on the doorknob, he thought of the savage and bitter anger that had boiled up inside him when he had been fighting those two men. For the third time since this trouble had started, he seemed to be seeing himself with a sharper sense of perspective and he knew that the taint of violence that had been born in him that night when the citizens of this town had turned against him had never left him. It was still there, something painted over his soul, something which would be with him until Ed Chapman was dead.

He did not hesitate once that thought, once the realisation passed through his mind. He expected trouble now and was determined to meet it more than half way. Jerking open the door, he stepped out into the street, blinking for a moment in the strong, almost blinding sunlight that flooded down on him. For a second the red haze was back again, searing across his eyeballs. Then he could see clearly once more and he started forward along the street, walking carefully in the exact centre, eyes flicking warily from side to side, alert and watchful for the first movement that would warn him there was trouble lying in wait for him.

He knew by some strange instinct deep within him that Ed Chapman was not far away. The gunman who lay in that house near the bank beside the unconscious form of Chet Wainwright said he had been sent there to bring him along to Chapman. That meant he had to be somewhere around — and close. He would not want to be too far away, just in case of trouble.

At the far end of the street he could make out the bunch of riders who had wheeled their mounts and were just beginning to walk them back along the main street towards the middle of town, but they were the best part of a quarter of a mile away yet, and he knew that if luck remained with him, he would spot Ed Chapman before those horsemen were in a position to interfere. Once he had evened the score with the gunslick, he cared little what happened to him. He would have finished what he had set out to do. The rest would be up to the townsfolk, and this time Chet Wain-wright would not be there to lead them on to murder.

The movement, when it came, was

unexpected. His averted vision caught the slight movement to his left. Chapman must have been watching the front of the house all the time, waiting for his companion to bring him out into the street. When he had noticed Matt come out alone, he had known that his plans had somehow gone astray and that he would have to finish Matt himself. The stabbing flash of gunfire came a split second later and the bullet hummed viciously through the air close to Matt's head as he flung himself instinctively to one side, rolling over and over in the white dust of the street, getting his feet under him and thrusting himself upright, scuttling crabwise for the opposite side of the street, where he threw himself flat on to his face on the wooden boardwalk. Two men on the street ran for cover as Chapman fired again, the bullet thudding into the wooden upright near Matt's body, tearing huge slices from them.

He swung round, caught a fragmentary glimpse of the other lying prone behind the water trough almost directly opposite him. Snapping a couple of shots at the other, he heard them strike the stone of the trough and go shrieking off into the distance. Chapman pulled his head down out of sight.

At the end of the street, alerted by the burst of gunfire, the riders were spurring their mounts forward. Matt eyed them for an instant from the corner of his vision, then switched his attention back to Chapman. He doubted if there would be any trouble from the riders. They would not step in until one man lay dead.

A slug scorched his cheek, and he cursed himself for letting his attention wander, even for a second. He made out the scrape of the other's body on the boardwalk as he tried to shift position. Clearly, Chapman was not as hard a man as he had liked to make out. He had less pure nerve than Clayburn. Once he got his legs under him, he tried to ease himself forward. Matt held his fire as he saw the other's shadow lengthen as he tried to push himself upright at the back of the trough. He laid his gun against the shadow and held it there to get a better aim as soon as the other's nerve broke completely.

'You don't stand a chance, Turner.' Chapman yelled the threat at the top of his voice. He still crouched down, not daring to show himself. 'You've got the whole of this town on your trail. Why don't you give yourself up? They'll give you a fair trial.'

Matt gave a cynical laugh. 'Like they did after I'd been arrested on that trumped-up charge? You framed me, Chapman, and I swore then that I'd kill you.'

Even as he spoke, as if his words had been a prearranged signal, the other suddenly lurched forward, sent a couple of shots smashing in Matt's direction, ran out into the middle of the street, twisting to face Matt as the other rose to his feet. Deliberately, Matt stepped down from the sidewalk and advanced towards the other. There was a confused shouting in the near distance, but he forced himself to ignore it completely. All that mattered now in the world was the man in front of him. It was as if they were the only two people in the whole world, as if everything else had suddenly faded away. He saw the look on the gunman's heavily jowled features, saw the sudden tightening of his lips as determination stiffened his will.

Chapman brought up the gun in his right hand, the barrel jerked above the line of fire. It needed only the quick downward thrust of his wrist, a quick snap to bring the barrel into line, then the pressure on the trigger, to send the bullet tearing into his body.

'Draw, damn you, Chapman!' Matt yelled thinly.

His gaze was fixed intently on the other's face. It was always possible to tell from the swift change of expression when a man meant to pull the trigger, and a moment later he saw the glint of purpose harden abruptly. His own gun spoke a split second before Chapman's. He saw the gunman stagger under the impact of the lead, saw the spreading stain of red on the man's shirt as the expression on his face changed to one of stupefied amazement, muscles of his face loosening as he died on his feet.

As he toppled forward into the dust of the street, his own gun went off and the bullet ploughed a neat furrow in the dirt beside Matt's foot.

For a moment, Matt stood there, unmoving, staring down at the inert body of the killer stretched out in the dust. Then he pouched his gun and lifted his head to fasten his gaze on the men who sat their horses only a few yards away. He heard the unmistakable click of a gun being cocked and there was an immediate coldness and stillness inside him.

Saddle leather creaked ominously as men shifted their weight a little. Hooves stomped in the dust, and a rifle and several guns were lined up on him, glinting in the strong sunlight.

This could be the end of trail for him, he thought quickly. No sense in trying to go for his own guns and take on this bunch. They would shoot him down before he pulled guns clear of leather. He stared up into their faces and saw no pity there.

Then, abruptly, behind him, a voice ordered:

'All right, hold your triggers.'

He turned. Sheriff Hogan moved forward. His eyes took in Chapman's sprawled body, then switched to Matt's face, and he thought he saw a faint smile on the lawman's face.

'There's the man who organised the attack on the stage.' Hogan pointed down at the dead man lying in the middle of the street. 'Ed Chapman and his two brothers were the brains behind it all. They had Clayburn and Gorson in it with them, and they framed this man for the hold-up.'

'You got any proof of this, Sheriff?' asked one of the men. He pushed his mount forward a little way. 'Chet Wainwright seemed pretty sure that — '

'Chet Wainwright was in it with them. He had no part in the stage hold-up, but he was the man who had agreed to get rid of that gold bullion for them. They couldn't get rid of it themselves. That's why he wanted Turner here hung that night when I arrested him.'

'But why should they frame Turner for it?' demanded another man harshly.

'Reckon you can tell 'em that.' Hogan turned to Matt, who nodded slowly.

'I gave evidence against this gang some years ago in Tucson,' he said quietly. 'They swore they'd get me, and when they busted out of jail there and rode west, this was the way they figured to do it.'

Hogan gave a brusque nod. 'Your friend, Doc Parsons, warned me where you'd gone,' he said softly. 'He seemed to think that you were walking into a trap and that you'd need help.' A wry grin twisted his lips. 'Seems he was wrong on that score, but I went straight to Wainwright's place and found him there with that other killer. Maybe you figured you'd killed 'em both, but they're still alive and they talked. What they said clears you of any complicity in the hold-up, or the shooting.'

Matt let the air go from his lungs in a long, drawn-out sigh. For the first time there was a sense of peace in his body, but he could scarcely believe it. He still had the feeling that he was dreaming all this, that he would wake up and find that he was still a wanted man, still a hunted criminal.

He watched as a couple of men came forward and picked up the body of the gunman, carrying it to the side of the street.

Hogan turned to him. 'What do you figure on doing now, Matt?'

The other shrugged. 'I'm not sure. I still have that feeling there's a price on my head, that I have to keep running, or I'll get a slug in my back from some posse.'

Hogan took him by the arms, led him forward. 'My advice is to put up your gun and try to forget that this ever happened. I know that it won't be easy, but if you want to go on living, it's something you'll have to do, or you'll have every gunslick who fancies himself as quick on the trigger coming after you, determined to set himself up against the man who finished the Chapman gang single-handed.'

Matt nodded slowly, wearily.

'I figure that's good advice,' he murmured. 'Right now, I'd like to get away from it all, get away from this town.'

'Got any place in mind?' The other looked at him sharply.

'Maybe.' Matt forced a grin. There were a lot of thoughts and memories stirring deep within him. 'You want me here for anything, Sheriff?'

'Nope.' The other regarded him evenly for a long moment. 'I figure this just about cleans up the trouble here in Saddlerock.'

'Then I'll be riding out.'

* * *

There was a hot wind blowing along the trail as he rode out of town and headed east. Far on the horizon, the thunder-heads were beginning to push up from the ground, piling high against the hazy whiteness of the sky. He eyed them curiously for a moment, then gigged his mount, raking spurs along the animal's flanks, urging it forward. He would have to hurry along the trail if he didn't want to get wet.

He rode with a new feeling in his mind now, a sense of freedom which he had thought was gone for ever. A couple of miles from town he came to the timber country, passed over the low crests, and then reached the summit of the trail, pausing there to glance down over the wide, stretching country that lay spread out below him. The sun had already passed its zenith, was tracing its downward curve to the west, but long before it reached the horizon it would be blotted out by the rising thunderheads.

Setting his mount to the downgrade, he felt the excitement rising inside his mind. Reaching the flatness of the prairie, he set his mount to the north-east, eyes searching the wide horizons until they picked out the small ranch-house set at the end of the lush green valley between the rolling hills. For some strange reason he slowed the gait of his mount, suddenly unsure of himself. He did not know what to expect here. Maybe he had been merely thinking about what could happen and it had been nothing more than wishful thinking on his part. A man rode with strange ideas after he had been so long on the trail alone.

He rode into the small courtyard, the sound of the sorrel's hooves on the hard-packed dirt echoing dully. Reining his mount, he sat absolutely still for a moment. Then the door of the ranch opened and he saw her standing in the opening, staring out at him as if unable to believe her eyes. Then she was running towards him as he slid from the saddle and stood, waiting. Then she was in his arms, her face pressed hard into his chest, her voice muffled, as she said:

'Don't you ever make me go through that again, Matt Turner — ever again.'.

THE END

We do hope that you have enjoyed reading this large print book.

Did you know that all of our titles are available for purchase?

We publish a wide range of high quality large print books including:
Romances, Mysteries, Classics General Fiction Non Fiction and Westerns

Special interest titles available in large print are:
The Little Oxford Dictionary Music Book, Song Book Hymn Book, Service Book

Also available from us courtesy of Oxford University Press:
Young Readers' Dictionary (large print edition) Young Readers' Thesaurus (large print edition)

For further information or a free brochure, please contact us at:
**Ulverscroft Large Print Books Ltd., The Green, Bradgate Road, Anstey, Leicester, LE7 7FU, England.
Tel:** (00 44) 0116 236 4325
Fax: (00 44) 0116 234 0205

Other titles in the
Linford Western Library:

GAMBLER'S BULLETS

Robert Lane

The conquering of the American west threw up men with all the virtues and vices. The men of vision, ready to work hard to build a better life, were in the majority. But there were also work-shy gamblers, robbers and killers. Amongst these ne'er-do-wells were Melvyn Revett, Trevor Younis and Wilf Murray. But two determined men — Curtis Tyson and Neville Gough — took to the trail, and not until their last bullets were spent would they give up the fight against the lawless trio.

MIDNIGHT LYNCHING

Terry Murphy

When Ruby Malone's husband is lynched by a sheriff's posse, Wells Fargo investigator Asa Harker goes after the beautiful widow expecting her to lead him to the vast sum of money stolen from his company. But Ruby has gone on the outlaw trail with the handsome, young Ben Whitman. Worse still, Harker finds he must deal with a crooked sheriff. Without help, it looks as if he will not only fail to recover the stolen money but also lose his life into the bargain.

THE WIND WAGON

Troy Howard

Sheriff Al Corning was as tough as they came and with his four seasoned deputies he kept the peace in Laramie — at least until the squatters came. To fend off starvation, the settlers took some cattle off the cowmen, including Jonas Lefler. A hard, unforgiving man, Lefler retaliated with lynchings. Things got worse when one of the squatters revealed he was a former Texas lawman — and no mean shooter. Could Sheriff Corning prevent further bloodshed?

CABEL

Paul K. McAfee

Josh Cabel returned home from the Civil War to find his family all murdered by rioting members of Quantrill's band. The hunt for the killers led Josh to Colorado City where, after months of searching, he finally settled down to work on a ranch nearby. He saved the life of an Indian, who led him to a cache of weapons waiting for Sitting Bull's attack on the Whites. His involvement threw Cabel into grave danger. When the final confrontation came, who had the fastest — and deadlier — draw?

BLACK RIVER

Adam Wright

John Dyer has come to the insignificant little town of Black River to destroy the last living reminder of his dark past. He has come to kill. Jack Hart is determined to stop him. Only he knows the terrible truth that has driven Dyer here, and he knows that only he can beat Dyer in a gunfight. Ex-lawman Brad Harris is after Dyer too — to avenge his family. The stage is set for madness, death and vengeance.